LA

Intermezzo

Spirit Matters

Wisteria Tearoom Mysteries

INTERMEZZO

SPIRIT MATTERS

A Wisteria Tearoom Interlude

Patrice Greenwood

Evennight Books/Book View Café
Cedar Crest, New Mexico

This is a work of fiction. All of the characters, organizations, and events portrayed in this novel are either products of the author's imagination or are used fictitiously.

INTERMEZZO: SPIRIT MATTERS

Copyright © 2017 by Patrice Greenwood

An Evennight Book
Published by Book View Café Publishing Cooperative
P.O. Box 1624
Cedar Crest, NM 87008

www.bookviewcafe.com

Cover photo: Chris Krohn
Piano courtesy of Darragh Nagle

ISBN: 978-1-61138-689-9

First Edition July 2017

for Sherwood

who demanded it

Acknowledgments

My thanks to the following wonderful people for their help with this book: Pari Noskin, Sherwood Smith, Darragh Nagle, and Chris Krohn; and to my colleagues in Book View Café.

A Note from the Author

Dear Readers,

This book is a little different. I'd like to explain a few things so you'll know what to expect.

~ This is not the next Wisteria Tearoom Mystery. That will be *As Red as Any Blood*, coming out in the fall of 2017.

~ This is not a novel, it's a novella, about a third as long as the novels. Cheer up! You'll still get a full-length novel later this year.

~ This is not a murder mystery. It's material that I wanted to put into *A Masquerade of Muertos*, but if I had done so it would have slowed the main story too much.

~ Finally, if you have not encountered the Wisteria Tearoom books before, this is not the best one to start with. If you haven't read book 5, it might not make a lot of sense to you. Any of the mysteries is a better choice. Since they're sequential, I recommend starting with book 1, *A Fatal Twist of Lemon*.

I hope you enjoy this little interlude. Meanwhile, I'm off to the writing chair to work on book 6.

—Patrice Greenwood

A MESSAGE POPPED UP ON MY COMPUTER SCREEN:

> Willow Lane's on line one. Do
> you want to take it?

Kris, my office manager, was at her desk in the adjacent office and could have called out to me, but I dislike shouting from room to room so we had developed the habit of sending internet messages. I winced as I read this latest one. At least she couldn't see me.

> Yes, thanks.

Not for the first time, I wished there was a physical door between our offices that I could close for privacy's sake, instead of our shared doorway out into the upstairs hall. I was eager to talk to Willow – even more so than I'd been when we'd agreed to arrange a meeting – but I didn't want Kris, whose boyfriend had been killed just a couple of days earlier, to overhear our discussion.

The phone chirped and I picked up the handset.

"Willow, hi," I said. "Thanks for getting back to me."

"I heard about your employee finding a body in Hidalgo Plaza on Saturday night," she said, her voice cool and collected as usual. "Is there anything you want to tell me?"

"Yes, but not now," I said, glancing toward the doorway. "Would tomorrow afternoon work for you?"

"Sure. I assume you still want to discuss the lights you saw last week."

"Yes, yes! It's all related."

"Ah. Well, do you want to meet at Hidalgo Plaza, or should I come to the tearoom?"

"Let's meet there. Two o'clock?"

"Two-thirty would be better. I'm giving a tour at noon."

"Two-thirty it is. See you then."

I hung up with a small sigh of relief. The last thing I wanted was for Kris to hear what Willow and I would be talking about. Willow's profession leading spirit tours in Santa Fe still bothered me a bit, though I couldn't deny that the "Spirit Tour and Tea" events we'd held in October had been a boon to the tearoom's bottom line. I'd gotten to know her a little better, and I was now convinced that she wasn't hallucinating or a crackpot, but I still preferred to keep my request for her advice quiet.

Because I wasn't sure that *I* was not hallucinating.

Kris came to the doorway with a handful of

papers, and I was struck by how tired she looked. The black baggy tunic over jeans was far from her usual elegant style. Her hair—normally a glossy, black waterfall—was caught back in a peremptory ponytail, and her face was even more pale than usual. She hadn't bothered with makeup, I realized. Normally she *always* looked perfect at work, even on a Monday, such as today, when the tearoom was closed.

"Payroll's ready for you to sign," she said, gesturing with the papers.

"Thanks." I held out my hand and she came forward to give me the pages of printed checks. As she turned away I added, "Want to take a break and have a cup of tea?"

She shook her head. "Thanks, but I'd rather keep busy. I'm working on the newsletter."

"OK."

I watched her vanish back into her office, wishing I could do something to lift her spirits, and knowing that sometimes that isn't possible when someone is grieving. I'd been there, I knew how it felt. Both my parents were gone, and there were still days when I just had to focus on getting through one task at a time.

I had offered Kris the day off, and she'd declined. I knew better than to press it; she probably needed the distraction of work to keep her mind off her loss.

Kris hadn't been romantically involved with Gabriel for very long, but she'd apparently known him for several years. His accidental death by hanging had sent a shock wave through her circle of Goth friends. Gabriel was charismatic and amazingly talented, and his artistic career had just begun to take off. Such a tragedy. I had only met him recently myself, yet I found my older grief all too easily awakened by his death.

Shaking away the sadness, I picked up a pen and began signing checks. Lots of overtime this time, because of the Halloween party that Kris and her friends had thrown at the tearoom, which had ended so tragically. I looked closely at Kris's hours to make sure she hadn't shortchanged herself.

When I'd signed the checks, I took them into Kris's office and laid them in her "IN" box. She nodded without looking away from her monitor. Not wanting to break her concentration, I collected the empty teapot from my credenza and went downstairs to brew a fresh pot. Kris might not want tea, but I did, and the kind I wanted was downstairs in the butler's pantry.

It was almost four, and the downstairs was empty. Julio had been in the kitchen that morning, but had gone home when his prep for the week was done. The house was quiet except for the wind blustering around outside. I shivered, regretting the absence of fires in the fireplaces, and went into the pantry.

While the kettle rumbled, I set up the teapot with pu-erh, a rather exotic, fermented tea that was something of an acquired taste. I adored it, and Kris was warming to it although her favorite was still Lapsang Souchong.

The lace curtains were pulled back from the pantry's window. Through the glass I watched the cottonwood branches dancing in the wind, leaves flying. November now, and there were more leaves on the ground than left in the trees.

November the 2nd, I realized. All Souls Day, Julio had told me. In the *Dias de los Muertos* tradition, it was a day to visit the cemetery and decorate the graves of one's ancestors. Watching the gusts of wind in the garden, I decided another year would be better for exploring that tradition.

With a couple of minutes left on the timer, I went into the kitchen to forage for something to nibble with my tea. There was leftover *pan de muerto* in the fridge. I took out one of the sugared buns, added some butter to the plate, and put it on a tray with a violet chintz teacup and saucer. The timer went off and I collected the tea, then carried the tray to the Violet alcove.

All the draperies from the party had been removed, and all the furniture restored to its proper place. On the mantel, an array of sugar skulls— tribute to Vi Benning—lay beneath her portrait. A votive candle burned in a glass holder in the center of the mantel, on a stone coaster I'd put beneath the glass for safety reasons. To one side, another votive stood, also on a coaster. Leaning against the wall behind this candle was a photograph of Gabriel Rhodes, dressed in black, smiling.

My throat tightened. Had Kris added this little memorial to what had become an undeniable *ofrenda?*

I looked from Gabriel to the portrait that Julio had painted of Vi. They had never met, as far as I knew.

I really should not let this alcove become a permanent shrine to the dead. Gabriel's picture could stay until tomorrow morning, but then it would have to come down, along with all the skulls.

I picked up the sugar skull I had decorated for Vi and set it on the low table before the two wing chairs, where it could watch me pour my tea. With a sigh I settled into my chair and sipped the pu-erh, enjoying its rich, complex flavor.

A spatter of rain made me look toward the window. The garden was getting dark, though it was barely past four. I glanced at the fireplace, wishing again for a fire. I *could* build one. It was my house, after all. A fire would warm up the chimney, which would warm up my bedroom upstairs.

Unwilling to leave my cozy wing chair, I settled for a second cup of tea and a bit of *pan* slathered with butter. As I savored the soft, orange-flavored bread, my gaze drifted to Gabriel's photo again, and my thoughts to the flashes of light I had seen in Hidalgo Plaza, just days before he had died there.

If I had been able to meet with Willow before the Halloween party, could I have prevented his death?

I would never know. I closed my eyes, admonishing myself. Gabriel's death was *not* my fault. It was a tragic accident.

"Ellen?" Kris called from a distance.

I stood and went out to the hallway. Kris was by the back door, putting on her black leather gloves. She already had on her wool coat.

"I'm going home," she said, looking up as I joined her. "The newsletter draft is done. It's in your mailbox."

"Thanks. Sure you don't want to stay for a cup of tea?"

She shook her head, momentarily focused on straightening her sleeve. "No, thanks. Got a lot to do."

"All right. Stay warm."

She flashed a fleeting smile at me, then headed out into the chill. I locked the door behind her and returned to Violet.

Two days ago, Kris had been confident, strong, flushed with the excitement of a new love. Now she seemed...flattened. I'd never seen her so subdued.

Not to be wondered at. Still, I wished I could do something to make her feel even a little bit better.

I poured the last of the tea into my cup and savored it slowly. The flickering of the candles drew my attention to the mantel, where Gabriel's photo smiled into the gathering darkness. It was a lovely photo, without evoking any of the challenging points of his personality. Like many artists, he'd been fascinating, brilliant, and a bit difficult.

Dusk had fallen now, outside. I put my empty

cup on the tea tray, then added Gabriel's portrait and the votive candle. I didn't want to extinguish the flame that had been lit in his honor. Instead I carried it carefully upstairs, and placed it in the center of the low table by the front window. With the candle flickering before it, and all the sugar skulls I had decorated for my own remembrances around it, you couldn't be blamed for calling it a shrine.

~

Tuesday marked the start of our work week at the tearoom. Roused from hibernation by the smell of baking scones, I set about my daily routine with more determination than enthusiasm. I would have liked to stay snuggled under my comforter—for, say, a week—but duty called.

The weather was cold, with a brisk breeze blowing. I found great satisfaction in asking Rosa and Iz to build fires in the parlor fireplaces, and used the excuse of clearing away the sugar skulls to snatch a few moments enjoying the fire in Violet before we opened for the day. I left the votive before Vi's portrait, and made a mental note to get a quote for having better lighting for the painting installed.

Kris showed up on time, looking professional if still rather subdued. Her all-black ensemble was nothing unusual for her, but she wore no jewelry except for a pair of small, onyx stud earrings.

"You brought Gabriel's picture up," she said, standing in the doorway of my office.

I took a calming breath and rose, heading for the tea tray on the credenza. "Yes, and the sugar skulls for Vi, too. I put the ones you and Gabriel made on your desk. Would you like tea?"

She stared at me for the space of three breaths, looking a little hurt, a little angry. Then she swallowed.

"Yes, thanks."

I poured her a cup of Assam. "Business marches on," I said gently as I handed it to her. "I'm sorry if it seems too soon."

She shook her head and took a sip of tea. "I know. You're right."

"Gabriel's picture can stay up here as long as you like."

"Actually . . . could I put it in my office?"

"Of course."

She gave a fleeting smile and set down her cup, then fetched Gabriel's photo and the candle and placed them on her desk. She sat staring at the photo as I slid her teacup onto the desktop.

"I have a meeting in town this afternoon. Should I ask Nat to come in?"

Kris gave me an uncomprehending stare, then shook herself. "No. I'm OK. Tuesdays are slow."

They were. I spent the morning returning sugar skulls to those of my employees who had made them for Vi, and talking with them about the weekend's events. Rosa had not been present at the party, but her brother Ramon had been there, and she'd heard about it from him. She made no comment, but I got the distinct impression that her opinion of Goths had not improved.

Julio accepted his skull with a nod of resignation. His mind was elsewhere—the pumpkin fritters for the November menu were misbehaving—and I left him to his work.

Dee came in at noon, and would work until closing. I caught up with her in the back hallway, where she was donning her apron.

"I cleared away the skulls from Violet," I explained, handing her a storage bag containing the one she had decorated.

"Oh. Thanks," she said, tucking it into her cubby beside her purse. "How's Kris doing?"

"As well as one might expect."

Dee nodded, a slight crease between her brows. Then she squared her shoulders and smiled, ready to greet the customers.

Other than Kris, Dee had been the best acquainted with Gabriel of any of my staff. In the two weeks before his death, she had modeled for him as he painted the costume she would wear at the Halloween party.

She'd also found his body. She seemed to be holding up, so far, but I planned to keep an eye on her.

At two o'clock, I shut down my computer and looked in on Kris. "I'm off to that meeting, now."

She nodded and kept typing. I fetched my coat and hat, added a scarf for good measure, then left by the back door and headed for Hidalgo Plaza.

The air was chilly, and the breeze sharp enough to make me glad I'd dressed warmly. Leaves lay in restless drifts beside my driveway and swirled in the gutters of the streets. Autumn had turned gray, and winter was on its way in.

I was disappointed (but not surprised) to see electric "luminarias" already adorning the roofs of several buildings near the plaza. The Wisteria Tearoom, I had decided, would not put up holiday decorations until after Thanksgiving. Both Kris and my friend Gina had been trying to wheedle me into relenting on this edict, but I intended to stand firm.

The plaza was fairly quiet, with only a few dozen tourists and one busker: an accordion player. This was a slow time of year. Fiesta was long over and skiing wouldn't get underway until closer to Thanksgiving. Santa Fe didn't really have an off-season any more, but autumn and spring were less hectic than summer and winter.

As I reached the *zaguan* passage that gave onto Hidalgo Plaza from Palace Avenue, I hesitated, remembering the awful scene on Saturday night. Poor Dee, in her costume and skull face paint, had sheltered from the cold with me in that *zaguan* while she answered Tony Aragón's questions. All the while, cops were busy removing Gabriel's body from the iron hook where Dee had found him hanging over the garden. I'd had to identify him; he was also in costume, and his ID was back at the tearoom.

I shook off the memory and strode through the *zaguan*. The *plazuela* was quiet, the garden sad and fading. All the patio tables and chairs were stowed.

It was too cold to sit outside.

A woman in a long, black coat and gray scarf stood staring at the second story on the west side of the *plazuela*. Pale blond hair spilled from beneath a black hat, and I knew before seeing her face that she was Willow.

She heard me coming up the path and turned. "Hello, Ellen."

I summoned a smile. "Hi. Thanks for taking the time."

"Glad to. There are some interesting energies here."

I'll bet there are.

"Shall we look for some coffee?" I asked. "My treat."

"Yes, in a minute, but first please tell me about the lights."

I squared my shoulders, shoving my hands deeper into my coat pockets. "They looked like a flash of light from a crystal chandelier drop. I couldn't find a source for any of them."

Willow tilted her head. "Where did you see them?"

"The first one was out on the walkway, right by the entrance." I gestured, not wanting to go back through the *zaguan*, then tucked my hand back in my pocket. Willow nodded her understanding.

"The second one was here." I walked past her a couple of steps to the place where I'd seen the second flash of light. It was a junction of two small footpaths, just flagstones, that wandered through the garden. Dee had been standing on the spot when I arrived on Saturday night. I looked up, as she had been looking then, to the place where Gabriel had died.

"The third one was up there," I said, pointing toward the second story.

The hanging flower basket had been removed from the massive hook that Gabriel's lanyard had caught on. In fact, all the flower baskets had been removed. The garden was devoid of cheer.

"On the balcony, or on the hook?" Willow asked quietly.

She was well-informed. I recalled her telling me once that she had a friend in the police department.

"On the balcony," I said.

"Let's go up for a minute."

She started up the wooden stairs, and I followed. The balcony ran along the west side of the *plazuela*, and several shops opened onto it. Willow stopped at the point I had indicated, a space between two storefronts.

I joined her, remaining silent. She appeared to be listening as she gazed out over the *plazuela*, After a minute, she turned to me.

"One flash?"

I nodded. "One in each spot."

Her focus shifted to the hook. The balcony railing, ancient and made of wood, was too low for safety. Gabriel must have gone straight over it. If the hook hadn't caught him, he might have died from the fall.

Or he might not, but he would probably have been badly hurt. Not that it mattered.

Willow let out a sigh and pressed her lips together. "All right. Let's go inside."

We returned to the garden and crossed it. The fancy restaurant on the north side was closed until dinner hours, but the bistro on the east side was open. We went in past the long, polished oak bar and sat at a small table in the back. A sleepy waiter came to see what we wanted, took our orders for coffee, and left.

"Why did you say these lights were like a chandelier flash?" Willow asked, removing her hat and setting it on the empty chair beside her.

"Because I saw one a day or so later, and it was exactly the same."

"Saw one where?"

"In my dining parlor. You know—the chandelier there—"

Willow nodded. "Yes. Captain Dusenberry."

"Yes."

"Do you think the flashes here were sent by him?" Willow's gaze was direct and uncompromising, reminding me for an instant of Tony. I brushed that aside.

"It's the only thing that makes any kind of sense," I said slowly. "If they weren't sent by him, I don't know why they appeared."

"Why *do* you think they appeared?"

"Um. Well, maybe the captain was trying to warn me about ... what was going to happen. On Saturday."

"Why would he do that? What brought him here?"

I shrugged, feeling helpless. "I don't know. I was hoping you could tell me."

She gave a brief nod, then looked thoughtfully at the table top. The waiter returned with our coffees and glasses of water. He discreetly placed a bar menu by my elbow, then left us alone.

Willow drank some water, then folded her hands on the table and looked at me. "This is the first time Captain Dusenberry has manifested outside of the tearoom, that you know of."

It wasn't a question, but I nodded.

"And yet, his energy feels very familiar here," she said, reaching for her latté.

"Does it?"

"*Very* familiar. Almost as if it was a second home."

I picked up my cappuccino, but it was too hot to drink. After kissing the foam I put it back down.

"This was the Hidalgo family's home," I said.

"Yes. Are you aware of any connection between Captain Dusenberry and the Hidalgos?"

Well, there it was. Time to confess to my hoarding. "Yes. I found some letters."

Willow's delicate brows lifted slightly. "Letters?"

"From Maria Hidalgo to the captain. He saved them."

"Where did you find them?"

"Under the floor in the dining parlor."

"Which was his study."

"Yes."

"Interesting."

Willow drank some more water. Frowning slightly, she closed her eyes. I watched, fascinated. Was she communing with the dead?

"Oh," she said after a minute, opening her eyes. "He was courting her."

My heart gave a hard thump. I hadn't said anything that would lead Willow to conclude that. Even the letters didn't say anything about courtship; they were strictly friendly, though I was convinced that the Captain had loved Maria.

I sipped my still-too-hot coffee, burning my mouth. I put the cup down.

"Maria Hidalgo was an aristocrat, descended from the first Spanish settlers," I said. "Her family would have frowned on her being courted by an American army officer."

"Yes." Willow picked up her cup. "It must have made things difficult. Do you have copies of the captain's letters to Maria?"

I shook my head. "Only hers to him."

"May I see them?"

"Yes, but I didn't bring them. You'll have to come back to the house."

"Quite right. They should be preserved."

I ignored the pang to my conscience. She was absolutely correct.

"I'm planning to donate them to the museum, eventually."

Willow nodded but refrained from further comment, for which I was grateful. "This clarifies things," she said. "I've been wondering why Captain Dusenberry hasn't moved on. If he has unresolved feelings about a relationship with Maria, that may be part of what's keeping him close to Earth."

"I didn't know ghosts needed a reason to haunt people. I thought they just did it for fun." I took a cautious sip of coffee. It was cool enough now.

Willow shrugged. "Some low-level spirits enjoy malicious mischief, but Captain Dusenberry isn't like that."

"No. He's not malicious. He's the opposite, if anything—he's been helpful. That's why I'm wondering what he was trying to tell me with the lights."

She tilted her head, looking thoughtful. "You may be right that he was trying to tell you about … Saturday. Could be he was present because of his association with the location, and when you arrived he saw the potentiality for an event, and took advantage of your presence to manifest a sign acknowledging that."

"Wait—what? You lost me."

She sipped, then put down her cup. "If he was here, doing whatever he does here, and you arrived, he might then have noticed that a significant event for you was going to happen here soon."

"Ghosts can see the future?"

"They're not limited by our linear timeline. That's a physical-world thing. In the spirit realm, there's no time—not the way we perceive it. But they know that we're on a linear timeline, and they can communicate about events in our future or past if they choose to."

"OK," I said slowly, taking that in.

"So: you arrive here, the captain senses your presence and can see a significant event happening here for you. He decides to tell you about it, and the easiest way is to use the same manifestation he's created for you at the tearoom—the gleam of light from your chandelier."

"But there was nothing here to cast a gleam," I said.

"He probably borrowed some ether from you to create it."

"Wait. *What?*"

2

"CAN I GET YOU LADIES ANYTHING ELSE?" said the waiter, shuffling up to our table.

I froze, wondering how much he had heard. Willow, unfazed, gave him a pleasant smile. "Just the check. I think we're about ready to go."

She slid me a querying glance, and I nodded, then gulped some coffee. Willow picked up her cup and took a leisurely sip.

"You'll be wanting to check on your tearoom," she said. "Maybe we should continue this conversation there?"

"Yes," I said, grateful for her tact. "Did you say, 'ether'?"

"Not the chemical ether. There's another kind. I'll explain, but I really would like a peek at those letters before you close for the day."

"Sure."

The waiter returned with our check, which I paid. Willow and I donned our hats and coats, and stepped out into the *plazuela*, where the breeze had become a full-on, bitter wind.

"Did you drive?" Willow asked, turning to me.

"No, I walked."

She smiled and nodded toward the north *zaguan*. "I'll give you a ride."

She led me to the parking lot behind the plaza and a lush teal blue sedan. In a few minutes we were at my house, where Willow slid her car into the space beside mine. We hurried in through the back door and were met in the hall by Dee.

"Hi, Willow," she said, smiling. "Is there a tour today?"

"No, we've just been discussing some business," Willow said.

"Would you like me to make you some tea?" Dee asked, looking at me. "It's pretty slow."

"Yes, please," I said. "And bring up a couple of scones. We'll be in my office."

I led Willow upstairs. As we reached the top I paused, having heard something that sounded rather like a smothered sob. I glanced at Willow, who became absorbed in hanging her hat on the coat rack. I went on through the office doorway and looked in at Kris, who was at her desk, hastily gathering several tissues into a wad.

"Are you all right?" I asked.

She shot me a glance, and I saw that her eyes were red. "I'm fine," she said.

I looked away and unwound my scarf. "It's getting nasty outside. Not snowing yet, but feel free to go home early if you want to beat the traffic."

She was silent, and I snuck a peek at her face as I unbuttoned my coat. Kris sat frowning and blinking, hands clenched before her on the desk, apparently wrestling internally.

"Things are slow downstairs," I added, and went back to the hall, giving her space to decide.

Willow had hung up her coat and moved to the little sitting area by the window, where she was examining the sugar skulls. She looked up as I joined her.

"Some of these were in Violet, but not all of them," she said.

"Yes, I decorated several besides the one I did for Vi."

Willow nodded, gazing at my skulls. I heard footsteps on the stairs and went to meet Dee, relieving her of the tray she'd brought up.

"Thanks, Dee. All quiet below?"

She nodded. "Like a t- ... library." She shot a regretful glance toward the office, then went away. I brought the tea tray to the sitting area and slid it onto the table, shifting a couple of the skulls to make room.

"I think I recognize some of these," Willow said.

"Oh?" I picked up the teapot and poured.

I didn't really want to know if Willow had made contact with my parents or the murder victims I'd known. One ghost was enough for me.

"From the news," she added, and let it drop.

I handed her a cup and pushed the small plate of scones within her reach. "I'll get those letters."

"They can wait a bit. I was going to tell you about ether."

"Oh, yes." I poured tea for myself and took a scone. "Not the chemical."

"Yes. It's matter, but a different form of matter than what we're used to. It's less substantial. You may have heard of astral projection?"

I carefully spread lemon curd on half of my scone. "Yes."

"Well, the so-called astral body is made up of ether. It's sometimes referred to as the etheric double."

"So ... that's what ghosts are made of?" I asked, feeling out of my depth already, but game to follow along.

"Yes and no," Willow said. "The etheric double is actually discarded at death along with the physical body. Usually."

I didn't like that qualifier. With my mouth full of scone, I gave her a look of polite inquiry.

"Sometimes things go wrong," she said, "but that's not important to this discussion. The point I wanted to make is that we each have an etheric double, and the etheric matter that makes it up is more malleable than physical matter. For example, it can be used to create seemingly physical manifestations."

"Like a flash of light?" I said.

"Yes." Willow paused for a sip of tea. "In the late 19th century, when séances were all the rage, many of the manifestations that took place were created from ether by the visiting spirits."

"Flashes of light?"

"Usually more dramatic than that. One of the reasons there were a lot of manifestations in that era was that they were used to prove to the sitters in the circle that the spirits really did exist, that the human soul survives physical death."

"Oh," I said, and picked up my cup. I hadn't made up my mind about that question.

Or had I? I lived in a haunted house. I was, by now, absolutely convinced that Captain Dusenberry was real. That implied that I believed in the survival of the soul.

"A spirit could manifest an etheric hand, for example," Willow went on, "and use it to pick things up or to touch the people in the circle. Or a face, or sometimes even an entire body."

"Why didn't they just show their own bodies?"

"Because they didn't have bodies that could be made visible to people in the physical plane. Remember, the etheric double gets discarded. The spirits had to build a visible manifestation out of ether."

"So where did the ether come from?"

"Borrowed from the medium, usually. Or sometimes from more than one person in the circle, but the medium was the one who best understood what was going on."

"Borrowed from the medium...?" I was feeling lost again.

Willow set down her teacup and gave me a patient smile. "From his or her etheric double. With his or her permission, implied if not explicit."

I frowned and put down my empty cup. "You said Captain Dusenberry might have borrowed ether from me."

"Yes."

"But I'm not a medium."

Her lips curved in amusement. "Maybe you are."

"But I ... I didn't give my permission!"

"*You* might not have, but your higher self could have."

"My w*hat*?"

"I don't want to get too complicated, but you need to understand that only part of your soul is inhabiting your body. Your soul is a greater being, and that's often referred to as your higher self."

I was getting cranky. Too many new ideas. I'd heard the term "higher self" before but had never taken it seriously. Now Willow was asking me to do just that.

I reached for the teapot and refilled my cup. "So Captain Dusenberry could get permission from my higher self to use some of my ether, and I don't have a say?"

Willow smiled kindly. "Your higher self would never permit anything that's not for your greater good. Does it make you uncomfortable to think of Captain Dusenberry borrowing your ether?"

"Well, yeah!"

"You can ask him to stop, and he'll never bother you again."

I stared at her.

"Of course, there would be no more lights, no

more moving chandelier drops." She sipped her tea and returned the cup to the saucer. "It's up to you."

I put down the teapot. "That's it? I just ask him to stop? No exorcism required?"

Willow gave a soft laugh. "He's not a malicious spirit. If you ask, I think he'll respect your wishes."

Her words gave me a strange exhilaration, a feeling of unexpected power. I could get rid of the ghost, if I wanted to.

"I would miss him," Willow added. "Probably a lot of people would. But it's your house."

She was being very generous, telling me this. Captain Dusenberry was a prominent stop on her spirit tours. Not to mention that she and I had both made a nice profit on the tour-and-tea combos. Apparently she was willing to give all that up for the sake of my comfort.

I felt a little ashamed. I owed Captain Dusenberry a lot, not only because of the tours. He'd communicated with me before, trying to warn me about things. He'd also kept me company. There had been times when I'd felt miserable and alone, and he'd cheered me up by turning on the stereo, or the lights. Or both. A couple of times, he'd even played my mother's piano.

Of course, there had been occasions when he had done such things in circumstances that were ... inconvenient. Still, on the whole, I liked my ghost roommate.

"It's possible that he's still here trying to resolve something about his death, or about his romance with Maria Hidalgo," Willow said. "You could help him with that, and he might then move on."

"To heaven?"

"You could call it that. Heaven is a whole different discussion, and I think I've thrown enough at you for one day."

"You're saying he might go someplace else."

"I'm saying that heaven, or more accurately the afterlife, is more complex than most people realize."

I gazed at her, trying to understand all she had told me. It would take me a while to digest it, and she'd dropped some hints that I wasn't sure I liked.

"Do you believe in Hell?" I asked her in a small voice.

She looked out the window briefly, then gave a slight smile. "I believe we create our own hell."

That raised more questions, but I didn't have the courage to voice them. This was perhaps the most uncomfortable conversation I'd ever had with Willow. I followed her gaze to the window, and saw that it was snowing. Big fluffy flakes, tossed into swirls by the wind.

The sound of a desk drawer closing drew my attention to the office. Kris came out and took her coat from the coat rack.

"I'm taking you up on the offer to leave early," she said. "Can you do the deposit?"

"Sure." I stood, turning to Willow. "Will you excuse me for a moment?"

Willow nodded. I went over to Kris. Her cheeks were dry, but her brow was creased with strain. "Stay safe," I added.

She flashed me a small smile, glanced toward Willow, then flung an end of her black scarf around her neck and headed down the stairs. I followed, feeling mother-hen-ish, though I knew she'd resent any clucking. I watched through the lights around the back door as she got in her car, backed out, and drove down the driveway. When she was out of sight, I went into the butler's pantry, where Dee and Iz were putting away clean china. The wall clock read 4:44.

"It's snowing," I told them. "How many customers are left?"

"None, unless we get some walk-ins," Dee said. "The last reservation just left."

"We're closing early," I decided.

Iz shot me a grateful look. She had a bit of a drive to her family's house in Tesuque Pueblo.

"You can go as soon as you're done with that. Be careful going home," I told them, then went down the hall to lock the front door and turn around the sign to show "Closed." I turned off the gift shop lights for good measure, after collecting the day's receipts from the cash drawer.

Before going back upstairs, I looked into the kitchen. Mick was finishing the last of the dishes. He had his earbuds in, but looked up and gave me a thumbs-up and a grin, by which I inferred that his sister had told him we were closed for the day.

"It's coming down harder," I said to Willow as I reached the top of the stairs. "Do you need to go?"

"I've got all-wheel drive. I'll be fine. I'd really like to read those letters, if you don't mind."

"All right."

I fetched the letters from my desk, carefully setting aside the ancient ribbon with its dried rosebud. The small stack of yellowed, folded pages, I carried to Willow.

"Please keep them in the same order."

She nodded. "Of course." She laid the letters on the table before her and took a pair of reading glasses out of her purse.

"Do you need anything?" I asked.

"I'm fine. Thanks."

"Then I'll be in my office."

I left her to read while I balanced the day's receipts and made up the bank deposit. A very slow day; compared with most of October it was almost dead.

Why had I thought of that word?

Shaking it off, I locked the bank bag in my desk, then rejoined Willow. My teacup was there, full of tea that was now cold. I dumped it out and started a fresh pot. By the time I returned, Willow had finished the letters.

"What a lovely friendship they had," she said, straightening the little pile. "Thank you for letting me read these."

"You can read Spanish?"

"Pretty well, yes."

I gestured with the teapot, offering tea. She pushed her cup toward me.

"So, any insights?" I asked.

"Not immediately. I'll think about it. Have you done any research into Reynaldo?"

The last couple of letters mentioned Reynaldo, apparently a relative of Maria's. She had been concerned about his disapproval.

"No, I haven't followed up on that. I did check for Maria's papers, but the archives don't have anything."

"She probably destroyed them," Willow said. "Or if not, the family might have kept them."

That was something I hadn't thought of. "I wonder who would know about that."

Willow sipped her tea. "I think the Hidalgos still own Hidalgo Plaza. That might be a place to start."

I nodded. "I'll ask. And I'll check the archives for anything on Reynaldo," I said.

"Good. I'd love to hear about whatever you find."

My gaze drifted to the window, where the snow had stopped swirling and was now falling at an angle. With the storm to the west, it was prematurely dark.

"Would you like a demonstration of ether?" Willow asked.

I nearly dropped my teacup.

"Uh..."

"Not yours. Mine. It won't affect you."

"Um. OK."

Willow smiled, then put down her cup and got up to fetch her coat. She draped this over the back of her overstuffed arm chair seat and sat to one side of it, then held her hand in front of the black cloth.

"Watch my hand," she said, then closed her eyes

and took a long, slow breath, letting it out equally slowly.

I felt silly and embarrassed as I stared at Willow's motionless hand. Her manicure was immaculate, reminding me that I was overdue to freshen my own. Her fingers were slender and rather long. Good for piano playing, though she'd never mentioned any musical inclination.

"What do you see?" she said softly, recalling my wandering attention.

I bit back a sarcastic reply, and focused on her hand. I'd expected to be able to report nothing, but now I thought I saw the faintest cloudiness around her fingers and beyond her fingertips. I blinked and glanced toward the window. Despite the storm, the daylight coming through was brighter than the light from the chandelier behind us.

"There's a sort of fuzzy ... I don't know."

Willow nodded, then moved her hand, folding her splayed fingers except for the index finger. This she moved in a slow circle.

The cloudiness hadn't dispersed; instead, with the motion of her finger it coalesced into a little spiral: a tiny, spinning vortex. The back of my neck prickled.

"What do you see?" she said again.

I told her. She nodded and lowered her hand. The spiral remained for just an instant, then faded.

"How did you do that?" I asked.

"Concentration," she said. "But it's natural. We all use ether all the time. We're just unaware of it, because it's normal."

"We do? We are?"

"Sure. What do you do when you bang your elbow on something?"

I shrugged, then put one hand on the other elbow.

"Exactly. Ether can be used to heal. You've heard of 'laying on of hands,' right?"

"Yes."

"Entirely natural and normal. But we don't realize that we're using ether. We just do it."

I looked back at the space before Willow's coat. No trace left of the ether.

"So that—stuff—is what Captain Dusenberry used to make a flash of light?"

"Probably."

"And what he uses to turn things on and off?"

Willow nodded. "It doesn't take much ether to trip an electrical switch."

"What about the piano?"

"That would take a little more. Were the keys moving, or was it just the strings sounding?"

"Uh ... I didn't notice."

"I'm guessing the latter. It would take less pressure to move the hammer alone than to move a key. Less pressure means less effort and less ether required."

I polished off the tea in my cup and reached for the pot to refill it. "And he borrows the ether from me."

"Or from any willing person who's around. Contributing a small amount doesn't do any harm to the donor."

"Oh? What about a large amount?"

Willow picked up her teacup. "That doesn't happen very often, unless you're talking about a malicious or low-level spirit. They can draw on the medium too much, either from ignorance or irresponsibility, and that can result in exhaustion."

"That's all?"

"Usually all. Sometimes headaches, dizziness. Don't let this worry you. It isn't likely to happen with the kind of contact you've experienced. That kind of exhaustion is the result of extensive and prolonged drawing on a medium's ether, the sort of thing that might happen in a séance, when there are multiple and complex manifestations."

I took a swallow of tea. "Do you do séances?"

"Me? No." Willow chuckled. "If I want to communicate with a spirit, I usually just talk to them. Silently, mostly."

She talked to spirits. OK. That wasn't a big surprise, considering her profession.

"Do you do that often?" I asked.

"Not often, no. I don't like to intrude unless it's something important. It's not a séance, but it still requires a bit of effort on both sides."

"And what do you consider important?"

She smiled. "Helping solve a problem, usually."

I looked down at my cup. "Have you talked to Captain Dusenberry?"

"A couple of times. As I said, I don't like to intrude, and he's rather retiring."

I looked up at her, ignoring a flash of envy. "What did you talk to him about?"

A corner of her mouth twitched in amusement. "Well, the first time I came here I wanted to make sure he wouldn't cause you trouble. I just wanted to get a feel for him. We didn't actually talk." She sipped her tea, and added, "Spirits often don't use words, you see. They're more likely to communicate in emotions or ideas. Words have to be formed, or found, and that takes energy."

"Oh. So you couldn't just ask him who killed him?"

"I could ask, but the answer might not be straightforward. Or he might not know; remember, he was shot in the back."

"I've wondered if that's why he stayed around," I said. "If he wants to know who did it."

"I've wondered that, too."

The chandelier at the peak of the ceiling blinked off, then back on. We both looked over our shoulders at it.

"Brown-out," I said, a bit doubtfully.

"The light in your office stayed on."

I glanced toward my office, then back at Willow. She carefully put her teacup on the table and turned in her chair, looking up at the chandelier.

"Captain," she said gently, "if that was you, please blink the light again."

Off. On.

Holy crap!

I twisted around so I could see the chandelier. It was similar in style to the one in the dining parlor downstairs—very traditional, with five branches adorned with crystal drops—but it was both smaller in circumference and longer, hanging from the highest point in the upper hall's pitched ceiling. Nothing was moving.

"Thank you," Willow said. "If you would, please blink twice now."

The light obeyed. My breath came in short, almost-gasps. I put my cup on the table. It rattled in the saucer before I got it there.

"Please use one blink for yes, two blinks for no," Willow said, her gaze on the chandelier. "Do you know who killed you?"

Two blinks.

"Do you want to know?"

One blink.

Willow gave a slight nod. "Is that why you're still here?"

A pause, then three blinks. Willow looked at me.

"Yes and no?" I croaked, my throat dry.

"Probably." She looked back at the chandelier. "Captain, do you think we can find out who killed you?"

One blink.

"Can you tell us where to find that information?"

Two blinks.

"All right." Willow paused, appearing to muse over her next words. "Is there anything more you want to tell us now?"

Nothing. Then, a single blink.

We waited. Willow frowned in thought, her

attention shifting to the little pile of letters on the table before us.

"Something about Maria?" she said.

One blink.

"You loved her, didn't you?" I blurted.

Long pause, then one blink. I looked at Willow, who met my gaze.

"He may be getting tired," she said quietly. "This is a lot for one session."

I nodded, suddenly contrite. Had I wasted a rare chance, asking a question whose answer was obvious?

"Are there more letters?" Willow asked, returning her attention to the chandelier.

A pause, then one blink. I held my breath.

"Here in the house?"

Two blinks.

"In Hidalgo Plaza?"

One blink.

I covered my mouth with one hand to keep from shrieking. As it was, I gave a strangled squeak.

"We'll look for them," Willow said, glancing at me. "Is there anything else you want us to know now?"

Pause. Blink. And a second blink.

"All right. Thank you, Captain." Willow nodded, then closed her eyes. I watched her, keeping a nervous eye on the chandelier, but it didn't blink again and none of the drops had moved.

After a minute Willow took a deep breath, then

sighed and opened her eyes. Seeing me staring at her, she smiled.

"Well, that was interesting!"

"No—no kidding!" I said. "Oh, my God!"

"Maybe you should hold onto those letters a little longer. Just until we get this sorted out."

I nodded and picked up the little stack, cradling them in my lap. "There are *more*," I said.

"Yes. I should have asked whether they were letters Maria wrote, or ones he wrote. Maybe another time."

"You could ask now!" I said.

Willow shook her head. "I've said goodbye for now. Best let him be. He probably needs to rest."

I looked at the chandelier, wishing that wasn't so. "Did he use your, um, ether?" I asked.

"Most likely he borrowed from both of us," Willow said, reaching for her cup. "It's not something you actually feel, unless you're extraordinarily sensitive. Is there any tea left?"

I picked up the pot and poured for her, careful not to crush the letters in my lap.

"Thank you. Borrowing the ether was just part of it," Willow said. "Probably the smallest part. Manipulating it takes effort, even just to push it through an electrical line."

"So that's why he doesn't move the chandelier drops more often."

Willow nodded. "Disappointing as that is to our tour guests."

I gave a little gasp of laughter. Willow sipped her tea and smiled.

The adrenaline coursing through me began to dissipate. I picked up the letters.

"I'd better put these away."

"You might consider transcribing them," Willow called after me as I headed to my office. "You could read them aloud and record yourself, then work from the recording to keep from handling the letters too much."

"Good idea," I called back.

My hands trembled a little as I unlocked my desk. Not trusting myself to slide the ribbon back onto the letters, I laid it on top of them in the small box where I kept them, then locked them safely away.

When I returned to the hall, Willow was putting on her coat. "I'd better go," she said. "The snow isn't letting up."

I took her hat from the coat rack and held it out to her. "Be careful."

She smiled and put it on. I followed her downstairs to let her out, momentarily worried that Mick and Dee might have heard us, but Mick's car was gone; just mine and Willow's sat in the little parking area behind the house.

"Thank you, Willow," I said, unlocking the back door. "I can't thank you enough. I feel like I should pay you."

She waved a hand in dismissal. "No, no. This is interesting. Don't go to Hidalgo Plaza yet, all right? I'd like to do a little checking first."

I nodded.

"I'll call you. Thanks for the tea and the scone.

And the coffee earlier."

"Thank *you*," was all I managed to say. I watched her go to her car and drive away, then double-checked that I had locked the door, and turned toward the stairs.

The house was quiet, dark except for the lights in the hall and the stairwell. I looked toward the dining parlor, where I'd found the letters. The room where Captain Dusenberry had died.

The door stood open, as usual. The room was silent, dark.

"Thank you, Captain," I whispered.

I waited, holding my breath, but nothing changed. On a whim, I held up my hand in front of the darkened doorway and peered at it, looking for ether. After a few seconds I thought I saw a fuzzy outline, but then I realized I had shifted my gaze slightly. I shifted it again and confirmed that it was just an illusion; the fuzziness was outline of my fingers.

Collecting myself, I went upstairs, turning off lights as I progressed.

It was going to be hard to sleep.

THE NEXT MORNING, KRIS WAS LATE. It was so unlike her that I almost called, but there was the snow (fast melting now), so instead I made tea and sat at my desk and attacked the paperwork.

The never-ending stack of messages sat silently reproaching me. I looked through a few, answered a couple, then turned to the folder of candidates for the two part-time positions we had advertised for the holiday season: one server and one kitchen worker.

The kitchen worker would probably be a nice young Vietnamese college student, who had interviewed well and had a good, if short, résumé. As long as she passed muster with Julio, she was the obvious choice.

The server was a less clear-cut decision. There were three good candidates. I leaned toward hiring Dale Whittier, Kris's friend, simply because he had shown he could keep his head and act promptly during an emergency.

That was unfair to the other applicants, who had not had the opportunity to show me what they'd do when a depressed, drunken female tried to cut her own wrists in their presence. Still, I was pretty strongly inclined toward Dale. I felt I could trust him, even if (please, God) there were no more suicide attempts in the tearoom.

I pulled out his résumé and went over it again, looking for details I should consider more carefully. He was a Goth, of course. That wasn't on the résumé. It shouldn't influence me—his private life was none of my business—but I could hardly pretend I didn't know. Maybe the slight nervousness the knowledge gave me would serve to offset my appreciation for his quick thinking.

When I finally heard Kris's brisk step on the stairs, I glanced at my clock and saw that it was nearly ten. *Very* unlike her to be so late. I watched the doorway, hoping to gauge her mood from the glimpse I would catch of her as she went into her own office, but she surprised me and came into mine instead.

She still had on her coat. It was open, revealing a long knit tunic over leggings and boots, all black. Pretty casual for a work day, but there was the snow.

She looked as if she hadn't slept well. Dark circles were beginning to form beneath her eyes. Very Goth, but not like my poised, confident (if slightly cynical) business manager.

"Ellen," she said, sounding slightly out of breath, "I want to have a séance."

"Oh, Kris." I couldn't hide my dismay.

"After hours. We won't disrupt business, but it has to be in the dining parlor."

"I don't think it's a good idea—"

"I have to know," she said, then stopped abruptly, her face crumpling. Without another word she turned and went into her office, shrugging out of her coat.

Well, hell.

I rubbed my hands over my face and took a deep breath, then stood and went to the credenza. I poured tea into a clean cup for Kris, refilled my own cup while I was there, and carried both into her office.

She was sitting at her desk, wiping her eyes. Her coat hung sideways over the back of her guest chair, as if tossed there in haste. I put the teacups on her desk, carefully hung the coat on the coat rack out in the hall, then returned and sat across from Kris.

"What do you have to know?" I asked gently, picking up my cup and saucer.

She looked straight at me, eyes dry now, if a little red. "I have to know if Gabriel killed himself."

2~

"But it was an accident," I said.

Kris shook her head. "He might have jumped."

"But, Margo—"

"Margo was out of her mind. You know that."

"You're suggesting he jumped, just trusting that he'd be able to catch his lanyard on that iron hook?"

She picked up a pen and tapped the end against her desk, her mouth pressed into a thin line. "No. If he jumped, it was with the expectation that the fall would kill him."

"That isn't that likely," I said. "It was only one story."

"I didn't say it was a *reasonable* expectation."

"But Gabriel had no reason to kill himself."

Kris winced, as though I had twisted a knife. I waited. Finally she met my gaze.

"We argued," she said in a tight voice.

I nodded. I'd overheard a bit of it.

"I said some things...." She seemed unable to continue—just stared unseeing at her desk.

"Was it Dee?" I asked gently.

She pursed her lips, then shook her head. "It isn't Dee's fault. It was Gabriel, not her."

"Kris, I can't imagine your saying anything to make him want to die."

She looked at me, her mouth twisting wryly. "No?"

Her expression made me doubt. She could be sharp, even cruel. Ever since I'd hired her I'd wondered, at times, what past experience had given her the cynical streak she occasionally showed. Such moments were brief; even now, her face softened into grief.

"If I could just talk to him. I just want to set things straight."

"You don't think it's too late for that?"

"No!"

She banged a fist on her desk, making me jump and rattling her teacup, which landed askew in the saucer. She carefully straightened it.

"I have to know. A séance is the best way to find out. Please, Ellen."

"I'm surprised you haven't talked to Willow."

Kris grimaced. "I did. She won't do it. Even though she's the one...."

Abruptly, she picked up her teacup and took a swallow. "I heard her telling you about manifestations, and ether, and all that."

"Oh." I sipped my own tea. "You know, the chances of a manifestation are probably pretty slim."

"That's why it has to be *here*. Where he spent his last evening. A night he'd looked forward to, prepared for...." She paused, swallowed, and rubbed angrily at her eyes. "Anyway, I just want to try. I *have* to try."

I lifted my cup, but it was empty. I set it back down. "All right. After hours. But, Kris – I don't want any ... any dark ..."

"Black magic?" she supplied. "I'm not into that. Don't worry."

"If Willow won't do it, how are you going to...?"

"I have a couple of friends who are into spirit stuff."

This did not fill me with confidence. "When do you want to do it?"

"As soon as I can set it up. Tonight's probably out, but maybe tomorrow." With that, Kris turned to her computer, as if there were no more to be said.

I got up and carried my cup to the credenza for a refill. I had a day to get in touch with Willow and ask her advice—not about running a séance, but about making sure it didn't create havoc.

~

As the snow melted under a cheerful November sun, the tearoom began to bustle. The cold weather had apparently inspired Santa Feans with a desire to get out and about. We had more walk-ins than usual, and I ended up helping downstairs for most of the day. True, I was partly giving Kris space, and partly avoiding further discussion of the séance. I knew it was unlikely that Kris would give up the idea, and I shamelessly shoved it aside, to be dealt with later. I admit to wishing for some miracle to make her change her mind.

Gina Fiorelli, my best friend and incidentally my advertising agent, came by to whisk me away to a business lunch that we had scheduled before Halloween. Being a privileged person at the tearoom, she was allowed by my staff to come upstairs unescorted, and she caught me leaving a voice message for Tony Aragón. When she appeared in my doorway in a scarlet coat over a magnificent paisley dress in shades of green and bronze, I hastily ended my message and reached into my desk for my purse.

"Happy November!" she said, enveloping me in an Estée-scented hug. "Let's get to The Shed before it fills up with tourists."

She hustled me into my coat and out to her car. I made a feeble protest that we could walk, but she overruled me on grounds of the weather, and drove the short distance along Marcy Street to the little lot behind Hidalgo Plaza, some of the closest parking to The Shed.

We entered through the north *zaguan*, one of three that gave access to the plaza. I couldn't help glancing at the balcony as we crossed toward the southwest *zaguan* and Palace Avenue.

Gina's heels clicked on the old bricks, wet now with melting snow. She got ahead of me as I paused to look at a doorway in the west side that I'd seen many times but never given much thought. It was an old, wooden door with glass panes in the upper half, set into the ground floor under the south end of the balcony. The wood was painted white, and the glass was shrouded by a shade on the inside. A brass plate reading "OFFICE" was mounted on the adobe wall beside it, and a small, hand-lettered sign taped to the lower right pane said "Back at 2:00."

"Hurry up," Gina called, "before the tourists eat all the soufflé!"

I hurried through the southwestern *zaguan* and caught up with her on the covered walkway between Hidalgo Plaza and the smaller *plazuela* that gave access to The Shed. My thoughts circled like windblown leaves around Captain Dusenberry, Maria Hidalgo, and Gabriel.

"What're you frowning about?" Gina said, clutching the pager given to us by the hostess, as we stepped into The Shed's small waiting room and gravitated to the little kiva fireplace. On this cold day, a fire burned brightly there, sending a bit of heat and some cheer into the room.

I shook my head, trying to erase the tension from my forehead. "Nothing, really."

Gina gave me a quizzical look. "Don't tell me there's another body."

"No! God, no. We're still dealing with the last one."

"I thought it was all wrapped up."

"Well—"

The pager in Gina's hand lit up and started playing music. We claimed our table and were led into one of the back rooms—through the passage where you have to duck your head to avoid hitting it on a centuries-old roof beam (much padded nowadays, and marked with a friendly sign with a picture of a duck, advising visitors to watch their heads). We settled in, ordered our lunch and a pair of Silver Coin margaritas, and drank a toast to a profitable holiday season.

"Now, what's bugging you?" Gina said. "Spill. I want your full attention for the ads, so get whatever it is off your chest."

I took a restorative sip of my Silver Coin. "Kris wants to have a séance."

"Oh yeah?" Gina grinned. "Can I come?"

I gave her an exasperated frown. "You're as bad as the Bird Woman!"

She laughed. "Remember the séance we had at that pajama party?"

"We were fifteen!"

Gina's eyes narrowed as she chuckled. "We all thought we were really talking to Cleopatra!"

"Until we caught Debbie Fisher pushing the pointer." I took a longer pull at my drink, feeling better. "I doubt Kris is planning to use a Ouija board."

"Who's she going to talk to? Gabriel, of course. Anyone else?"

"I sincerely hope not."

"You know, I wouldn't have thought Kris would go for that kind of thing. She's pretty level-headed, for a Goth."

"She's grieving. Grief makes you do weird things. It makes you grasp at straws."

"Yeah, but a séance?"

"She heard Willow telling me about them, and I guess the idea stuck in her brain. May I see the ads now?"

Gina opened her folio and poked at its contents. "Why was Willow telling you about séances?"

I swallowed some more alcohol. "She was explaining ether and manifestations."

She looked up at me. "Say what?"

I held Gina's gaze briefly. "Manifestations. Like what Captain Dusenberry does with the lights."

Gina leaned back in her chair. "What did Willow say about that?"

"Well, there's this substance called ether—it's not a physical substance, or not quite, but it can be used to make manifestations, and move things. I'm a little unclear on how it works."

"Sounds like baloney to me." Gina returned to fishing in her folio.

"No, it isn't. The captain turned on the chandelier while we were talking. And then Willow asked him to blink it once for yes, twice for no, and started asking him questions. And he answered!"

The excitement of communicating with the captain returned to me. Gina gave me a skeptical look.

"How do you know someone else wasn't flipping the switch?"

"We were alone in the house."

Her brows drew together in a frown. "Had you left Willow alone in the room before this happened?"

I blinked. "Maybe. I don't recall."

"She could have messed with the wiring. Plugged a remote control or something into the light switch."

"Gina!"

She shook her head. "It just sounds fishy to me."

"I thought you believed in Captain Dusenberry!" I said.

"I do. I'm just not sure I believe in Willow."

Our lunches arrived, putting an end to the subject. I ate a few bites of enchilada in silence, trying to remember my exact movements during my conversation with Willow by the upstairs window.

What would Willow have to gain from deceiving me? My credulity, was all I could think of, and since we had already done business together with the spirit-tour-and-tea thing, there was no need for her to persuade me.

Unless she had something more elaborate planned.

I tried, but couldn't think of any nefarious motive that would inspire her to hoax me. Plus, she couldn't have known that I'd ask her upstairs the previous day. Could she?

We mopped up the last of our enchilada sauce with bits of garlic bread, dismissed the plates, and ordered dessert. The Shed's famous lemon soufflé, baked in individual pots and served warm from the oven, was the obvious choice on a chilly day like this. While we waited, Gina spread printed drafts of my holiday advertising on the table between us.

The ads were nicely designed, but they didn't sing to me. I looked them over slowly, trying to figure out why. They had red and green ribbons and ornaments and all sorts of Christmasy images, along with teapots and teacups and people holding same while smiling.

"There's no food," I realized while staring at a lovely photo of candy canes and truffles beside a teapot. "We really ought to showcase Julio's food. It's our trademark."

"Wisterias are your trademark. What's wrong with the candy?"

"Nothing's wrong with it, but it could be any restaurant in town. I'd like to see something that's uniquely ours."

Gina sighed. "Our photographer's booked up for a week. If we have to change the pictures, we'll miss deadlines."

"Maybe just this one picture," I said, tapping the candy canes. "I can get a photographer and have Julio do some samples of the December items."

"By Friday?"

"I think so. I'm pretty sure."

Our soufflés arrived, and we gave them our full attention. I can't remember ever eating a lemon soufflé at The Shed without moaning at least once.

"Mm," Gina said after her third bite. "Food of the gods."

I nodded, my mouth full of warm, silky, lemony heaven. Gina scooped up another spoonful, then paused.

"OK, we can switch to a food shot. But if you don't have a usable photo by Friday, we'll have to go with this." She gestured with her spoon toward the candy photo.

"Deal," I said.

Mental note: call Kris's friend Owen, the photographer. (I liked his work.) Also, warn Julio that we'll need pretty samples of December food. Set it up for Thursday ... i.e., tomorrow.

"Yikes!" I whispered.

"Beg pardon?" Gina said.

"Nothing."

I scraped the last of my soufflé from my dish and savored it, permitted myself one small sigh of satiation, then pulled out my company credit card. This was a business lunch, and therefore deductible. We split the bill, and Gina dropped me off at the tearoom. I went straight into the kitchen, where Julio was just putting on his coat.

"I have a huge favor to ask," I told him.

A wary look came into his dark eyes. "What kind of favor?"

I explained about the ad, and that we'd need food for a photo session the next day. He frowned thoughtfully, then took off his coat. "I can do a batch of biscochitos now, and make some of the candy-cane scones tomorrow morning while I'm doing the regular ones for the day. Those should be pretty, with the crushed peppermint on top."

"You're my hero!" I kissed his cheek, which evoked a reluctant grin. "Clock back in. You're getting overtime for this."

He gave a small nod, as if to say, "Of course I am."

Of course he was. Julio knew his worth.

I wouldn't think about the budget—not now. I darted upstairs to my office and dug Owen Hughes's card out of my desk. I was in luck: he answered on the second ring. I told him what I wanted, and asked if he was available to take photographs the next day.

"I'm open until about five," he said.

"Excellent. Shall we say one o'clock?"

"Sure. See you then."

I said goodbye and put down the phone, relieved that it had all come together. Now if only we got a usable photo out of it.

We would, I told myself. Julio was a pro, and Owen was a marvelous photographer. At least ... with people, he was. I hoped that would carry over to food.

I checked my messages, hoping Tony had returned my call, but no luck. He was busy, I told myself. Probably a lot of paperwork to do after Gabriel's case. I shouldn't bother him.

I dialed his number. As it was ringing, I heard a knocking and looked up. Kris stood in the doorway.

"Got a minute?"

Tony's voice drew my attention, but it was his voicemail message. I put down my phone and gestured to my guest chair.

"Have a seat."

Kris sat and gripped the arms of the chair. "We're all set for tomorrow night. Seven o'clock."

"Tomorrow night?"

"The séance."

"Oh." I closed my eyes briefly. "Oh, yes. It has to be tomorrow?"

"The sooner the better. You don't have to be here if you don't want to."

"I'll be here." I smiled, hoping to reassure her. In fact, wild horses could not drag me out of my house while there was anything woo-woo going on inside. Captain Dusenberry would probably consider it cowardice if I left him to the mercy of the Goth crowd's séance, even if he wasn't the intended star of the show. This was his home as much as mine, the way I saw it.

"Thanks," Kris said. She stood and gave me a small, tight smile before going back to her office.

I wished I knew how to make her feel better, but I remembered all too well the kind of feelings she was having. When she was out of the room, I picked up my cell phone and brought up Willow's number. Biting my lip, I debated whether to reach out to her. Could Gina be right? Could she be deceiving me? I still couldn't think of any reason that would make such an elaborate hoax worth the effort.

And I didn't know anyone else who knew more about the spirit world. If she *was* a fake, she was a well-informed and competent one. She made her living at it, after all.

I sent her a text:

Kris wants seance. Help!

Taking my phone with me, I went downstairs to check on Julio and the biscochitos. The smell of warm cinnamon and sugar was already seeping into the hall from the kitchen. I slipped through the short hallway past the butler's pantry and found Julio taking a cookie sheet out of the oven.

He glanced up at me. "I made a couple of different shapes, since we hadn't decided."

"Perfect. Thank you."

"Can you put them away when they're cool, or should I stay?"

"Go," I said. "I'll take care of them. Oh, the photographer's coming at one tomorrow."

Julio nodded. "Scones'll be ready."

"Thank you, Julio!"

He took off his apron and hung it up, taking down his coat again. "You're welcome. *Hasta mañana.*"

I watched him leave, then looked at the cookies. Some were star-shaped, some crescent moons. We'd decided against the traditional fleur-de-lys shape as it was prone to breaking.

I could feel the heat rising from the pan, and smell the wonderful cinnamon sugar and just a hint of anise. It wasn't easy, but I resisted the urge to eat one.

Glancing toward the dish-washing station, I caught Mick eyeing the cookies. He gave me a sheepish grin and continued washing teacups. I left to make a round of the parlors.

It was just past four. Three parties were seated in the main parlor and enjoying their first cups of tea; one other group was lingering in Dahlia.

They would not have that option in December, as we had decided to institute a two-hour limit for reservations during the busy holiday season. Generous, I thought—two hours was plenty of time to consume a complete afternoon tea and indulge in deep conversation—but I knew there would be a few complaints. Some people resented change of any kind. Alas, we had bills to pay, and thus change was, in this case, inevitable.

I traded nods with Dee, on watch in the gift

shop, and headed upstairs. On the landing, my cell phone buzzed in my hand. I checked it and found a reply from Willow:

> I told her no.

I thumbed in an answer:

> She found someone else.
> Wants seance tomorrow
> night. What should I do?

> Let me make some inquiries.
> Hang tight.

Wondering what she would be inquiring about, and of whom, I went into my office and checked my messages on the house phone system. Nothing of interest. I was tempted to send Tony a text, but I knew he was angry with me, so it wouldn't help. I'd just have to let him cool down.

Like the biscochitos.

Sighing, I sent an email to my contact at the State Historical Archives, requesting information about Reynaldo Hidalgo, then busied myself with the dreaded message-slip stack. When I'd dealt with six of them, I got up to reward myself with a fresh pot of tea.

"Is Julio making biscochitos?" Kris called from her office as I collected the teapot.

"Yes. For a photo shoot tomorrow. They're off limits."

"Dang. It's giving me the munchies."

"You're not alone."

We were used to tempting aromas wafting up

the stairwell, but there was nothing more mouth-watering than the smell of fresh biscochitos. I made tea, drank some, was still unsatisfied, and decided it was time to check whether the cookies were cool enough to store.

I found Mick clocking out. Clean china sat gently steaming in the drying rack. The biscochitos lay innocently on their sheet, still emitting a hint of their silent siren's call.

Dee came in, removing her white apron.

"Last party gone?" I asked her.

She nodded, dropping the apron in the laundry hamper. "I locked the front." She looked toward the cookies, her neck elongating a little and her nostrils delicately flaring.

"Thanks," I said, and handed her and her brother a still-warm biscochito apiece.

"Mmm! Thank you, Ellen!" Dee said, and bit into hers.

Mick broke into a grin. "Thanks, boss. The smell's been driving me crazy."

I saw them out and locked the back door, then returned to the kitchen and permitted myself one biscochito, letting small bites melt in my mouth while I put the rest away in a container. I kept one out for Kris, and carried it up to her along with the day's receipts.

She accepted the napkin-wrapped cookie and stared at it while I laid the bank bag on her desk. Then she burst into tears.

"Oh, Kris." I sat in her guest chair, watching her rub at her eyes.

"It's nothing," she said soggily. "It's ... I can't explain."

"You don't have to." I smiled gently. "I'll be at my desk if you need to talk."

"Thanks," she whispered.

I glanced back from the doorway in time to see her take a bite of biscochito. She'd be all right.

Back at my desk with a fresh cup of tea, I checked my phone and found a text from Willow.

> You should be OK. Best if I
> not be there but I can bring
> you some protection if you
> wish.

Protection? What, a spirit bodyguard or something?

> What kind of protection?

> Just some energy safeguards.
> OK if I stop by this evening?

I hesitated. "Protection" sounded like something out of a horror movie, something that was bound to fail. I shook off the thought.

> Sure.

> Be there around 7.

I glanced at the clock: 6:15. Not enough time for dinner, but then I wasn't really hungry after my big lunch, not to mention the biscochito. I left the phone on my desk and went to the doorway into Kris's office.

She was staring at her computer, one hand on the mouse. I knocked on the door frame and she looked up.

"It's after six. We're closed."

Looking faintly surprised, she nodded and shut down the computer. "Bank's closed too. Should I put the deposit in night drop?"

"No, I'll take it tomorrow. I have an errand to run."

Kris nodded and got up, handing me the bank bag, which I put on my desk. I saw her out, and at the back door she surprised me by grabbing me in a fierce hug.

"Thanks, Ellen," she said roughly, then went out. I locked the door and watched her drive away.

The dining parlor, to my left, stood in darkness. Faint light came through the lace curtains and shone softly on the crystals of the chandelier. On impulse, I stepped in.

A small gust of wind whuffed against the French doors. I hesitated while the shadows of the trees outside danced across the windows. I glanced up at the chandelier, but it was still.

This was the room where Captain Dusenberry had most often moved things. Specifically, the chandelier drops, and he liked to turn on the lights. He'd turned them on elsewhere in the tearoom, it was true, and he was partial to some of the classical music CDs in the stereo system.

But it was the chandelier drops that were his trademark. I smiled wryly.

"Captain, I hope this séance isn't going to

bother you."

I waited silently, watching the chandelier, but it remained still.

I hadn't actually asked a question. Maybe I should do that. Ask him to do "one for yes, two for no" again.

Something in me was reluctant. Fear of disappointment? Did I prefer uncertainty to knowing for sure that the Captain was a hoax?

I felt in my bones that he wasn't. He had played the piano to me—music that he knew I'd understand. I had told Willow that he'd turned on the stereo, but I couldn't recall ever discussing music with her.

But if she was part of some more elaborate scheme...if there were others in on it....

I shook my head. That was getting *truly* paranoid.

I went upstairs and changed out of my work clothes, then made a pot of herbal tea. I was just finishing the first cup when the back doorbell rang.

"Thanks for coming," I said as I let Willow in. "I feel kind of silly for bothering you."

"Oh, no, no," she said, smiling as she took off her coat. "Trust your instincts, Ellen."

She reached into a coat pocket and removed a small pouch made of black velvet. "I would offer to be present at the séance, except that I already told Kris I wouldn't do it."

"That's fine," I said. "I didn't mean to impose on you. I really just wanted some advice."

She cocked an eyebrow. "My advice is to stay as

calm as possible. Are you going to be there?"

"I think I'd better."

She nodded. "Then wear this."

She took a small pendant on a silver chain out of the pouch and offered it to me. It gave off a violet glint, and I saw that it was a dark crystal about an inch long, in a silver mounting.

"Amethyst?" I asked.

"Yes. Wear that while your, um, guests are in the house." She reached into the pouch again, this time extracting a little plastic bag filled with something white. "I assume Kris plans to use the study?"

It took me a second to recall that she meant the dining parlor, which had been the captain's study. Willow had called it that when we'd first met.

"Yes."

Willow turned to the room, opened the bag, and took out a pinch of the contents. "Sea salt," she said, noting my gaze.

I followed her into the dining parlor and around it as she trickled the salt against the baseboards. At each of the doors she reached up and put a pinch atop the frame. At the door that led into the main parlor she paused, looking thoughtful.

"May I open this?"

I realized I was holding my breath. Just beyond that door was the Rose alcove, where the seventh chamber—Gabriel's chamber—had been set up for the Halloween party. It was all gone, now—the cloth drapes had been removed and everything restored to its normal configuration. Willow could not have known about the party details.

Could she?

I nodded. Willow opened the door and stood before the empty frame, looking into the parlor. She was calm and watchful. I got the impression she was thinking intently.

Someone could have told her about the party. Kris, or Dee, or any of my staff who were there. Or any of the guests. But who would do that, and why?

I firmly invited my inner skeptic to have a seat and be quiet.

At last Willow poured salt along the threshold, then all along the top of the door as well. She gently closed it, added salt along the sills of the room's two windows, then sealed up the bag and returned it to the pouch.

"That's just to cleanse the room of any lingering darkness," Willow said. "It won't bother the captain. Is it all right if I place these in the corners?"

She held out her palm, showing me four smooth, polished, dark stones: irregular in shape, each about half an inch long.

"Apache tears," I said, reaching out to touch one. Willow didn't pull them away. "I used to have one of those when I was a kid."

"Obsidian is a good stone for warding."

I nodded. Warding sounded good, though I wasn't exactly sure what it meant.

I followed her again as she placed one stone on

the floor in each corner of the room. They disappeared in the shadows of the baseboards.

"These aren't going to disrupt what Kris and her friends are doing. If they summon something dark and powerful, it'll still come, but these should keep stray energies from being drawn to the circle."

I nodded as if I knew what she was talking about.

"Don't worry," Willow said with a smile. "Kris doesn't strike me as the sort who would dabble in darkness."

"She said she wouldn't."

"Does she speak for all her friends?"

I cleared my throat. "She said there wouldn't be any dark magic. I trust her."

Willow nodded, then looked slowly around the room. Finally she glanced up at the chandelier, and gave one more nod.

"Good. Please let me know how it goes." She went back to the hall and took down her coat.

"Thank you, Willow," I said, following. "What do I owe you?"

"I don't charge for this," she said with a gentle smile. She handed me the bag of salt. "In case someone sweeps in there before the séance. Just sprinkle it the way I did, if you need to."

"OK."

She shrugged into her coat and headed for the back door. "Oh, and I checked up on Hidalgo Plaza's background. No hauntings reported in the last several decades. If there were any restless spirits there, they've probably moved on. So you should be safe going back there to look into Maria's family history."

Possibly safer than I'd be in my own house that evening.

"Thanks," I said.

"Good luck! Call if you think of anything else you need from me."

"OK."

She paused to give me another warm smile. "You'll be fine. Nothing dark can influence you unless you give it permission."

I tried for a smile. "Well, I certainly won't do that!"

Willow nodded. "Good. Remember that."

When she was gone, I carried the salt and the amethyst up to my office and locked them in the top drawer of my desk along with the bank bag. I checked my messages. Nothing from Tony.

Well, in a way, that was good, because I had no idea how I would explain the séance to him. He'd be angry if he found out about it, because he would think it was stupid, and would hate the idea that people he respected took it seriously.

And maybe, just a little, because the unknown intimidated him.

I missed him. I knew he needed to cool down, but it was hard waiting.

A quiet evening would be good for me, I told myself as I crossed the hall to my suite. Some tomato soup, a good book, maybe a bath before bed.

I took my cell phone with me, just in case.

I SLEPT POORLY AND WOKE EARLY, smelling scones. Julio was back at it in the kitchen. I dressed and went down, finding him crushing candy canes with our largest rolling pin.

"Morning, boss," he called cheerily.

"Good morning. May I bum a cup of coffee?"

He paused and looked up at me. "You feeling OK?"

"Just had a rough night."

"Sure," he said, with a nod toward the coffee maker.

I helped myself and sipped black coffee while I watched him reduce the candy canes to red and white confetti. When a timer went off, he glanced at me.

"I'll get it," I said. "Got enough extras for me to have one?"

"Of course," he said as I slid off my stool and headed for the oven, "but those are plain ones."

"Plain is fine."

I pulled out a tray of hot, golden scones, put in a tray of unbaked ones that sat waiting on the counter, and reset the timer. I put one scone on a plate and added a dollop each of lemon curd and clotted cream from the fridge.

"Is that breakfast?" Julio said.

"Might have a candy cane for dessert," I said. "Or a biscochito," I added airily.

Julio frowned at me sidelong and ignored the bait. "There are oranges in the pantry. Help yourself to one."

"Thanks."

"Where are you taking these photos?"

"Good question." I looked around the kitchen, tempted to do it there, but I knew Gina wouldn't like the utilitarian background. "Maybe in one of the alcoves. I'll have to check what's free at one o'clock."

Julio nodded, then glanced toward the wall clock. I decided to get out of his way. I finished my coffee, put the mug in the dish-washing station, and carried my scone to the butler's pantry, where I started a pot of tea. While it was steeping I went up to the gift shop to check the reservations for the day.

One o'clock was fairly busy, but two adjacent alcoves were available: Dahlia and Violet. Tucked away behind the gift shop, they were our most private alcoves, and among the smallest. Those in the main parlor were requested much more frequently, although Violet was also beginning to develop a steady stream of requests.

I marked Dahlia and Violet as unavailable from one o'clock on, then carried my tea and scone to Violet. The hearth was cold, so I laid a small fire and lit it before settling back to have breakfast.

Gazing up at Julio's portrait of Vi as I sipped, I thought about the day ahead. I'd have to be here from noon onward, to deal with the photo shoot, but I'd be able to go out for an hour in the morning. That would be enough time to deal with the bank deposit, and also pay a visit to that little door marked "Office" in Hidalgo Plaza.

That thought made me a little nervous. I hadn't met any of the Hidalgos, but they were still a prominent family in Santa Fe. They might think my inquiry beneath their notice.

I had to try, though. Captain Dusenberry was counting on me. Heaven knew he'd waited long enough.

Looking at Vi's radiant face in the painting above the mantel, I wondered if she, too, had unfinished business.

In the distance, I heard the back door open and close. Staff were beginning to arrive. Time to get on with my day.

I finished my tea and carried the tray to the pantry, where Iz firmly relieved me of it. "Kris was looking for you," she said.

"Oh, she's here? Thanks."

It wasn't yet nine. Kris was early.

I went up and found her at her desk, eyes rather bright as she stared at the screen. She looked more herself today, in a long-sleeved black dress and her customary Goth-toned-down-for-work makeup. Still no jewelry.

"Good morning," I said from the doorway. "Do you want tea?"

"Morning. Sure," she said, intent on her computer.

I brewed us a fresh pot and poured a cup for Kris, leaving it at her elbow.

"I'm going out for a bit. I'll be back by noon."

She nodded, still typing. She seemed pretty normal except for an underlying buzz of energy. Anticipation, I guessed. Whatever happened with the séance, I hoped it would at least give her some closure.

I collected the bank bag, my phone (no messages), and my purse, and headed downstairs. In the hall I passed Iz, burdened with firewood for the parlors. In the kitchen, Julio was taking a tray of scones—peppermint, this time—out of the oven.

"I wasn't sure whether to put the candy on before the bake or right at the end," he said, lifting a pair of scones with a spatula and sliding them onto a small plate. "Tried it both ways. Which do you like better?"

He set the plate next to another with two similar scones, except that the candy was more melted on them. On the ones he'd just baked, the bits of peppermint still had edges.

"I think I like these better," I said, gesturing to the fresher ones.

"Me, too. Thanks. Do you need more than a dozen?"

"Probably not."

He nodded. "I'll box them and mark them once they're cool."

"Can you stay for the photo shoot?" I asked. "We might need some garnishing. You're more creative at that than I am."

"OK," he said, "but can I leave early tomorrow, then? Got a date."

"Yes, that's fair. Congratulations! I hope you're going someplace fun."

He laughed softly. "I'm taking my sister to a concert."

"That sounds fun," I said brightly.

Something in his expression told me he wasn't expecting it to be all that fun, so I refrained from asking for details.

"I'm off to the bank. Need me to pick up anything?"

Julio shook his head and turned to take down a mixing bowl, mind already on the next task. I headed out.

The day was sunny but cold. I drove to the bank, then headed back by way of Hidalgo Plaza, and was lucky enough to find a meter on the street. I had brought a hat for the occasion and now put it on. Not knowing who I'd meet in the little office, I hoped the formality would express my respect and sincerity.

Also, I liked hats.

I walked through the *zaguan*, cold enough to make me shiver, and into the dappled sunlight of the *plazuela*. Dry leaves had blown about the pathways. I went to the little white office door. It looked the same except that the hand-lettered sign was gone.

Deep breath. Straighten shoulders. I knocked.

Silence.

I was about to knock again when I heard a shuffling sound, perhaps a footstep. It came again and I waited, listening. At last the door opened with the clink of a bell hanging from the inside knob, and an elderly Hispanic man looked out. He was a little shorter than I and had thinning gray hair combed back from a high forehead. He wore a white dress shirt and a very nice bolo tie—with a chunk of turquoise that would probably pay for a small car—over black trousers. His eyes were dark and warm, and as he looked at me his expression changed from mild annoyance to mild interest.

I smiled. "Hello. I'm Ellen Rosings. I run a tearoom in an old house nearby, and I've been doing some historical research. Could you perhaps tell me anything about Maria Imelda Fuentes y Hidalgo?"

The man's silvered eyebrows rose. "Tia Maria. She was quite a character."

"Tia Maria?"

"Yes, that's what they called her. She never married. Would you like to see her picture?"

"Yes, very much!"

He stepped back, opening the door wider. "Come in. I'm Eduardo Hidalgo, by the way."

"Very pleased to meet you, Mr. Hidalgo," I said, and entered the office.

The room was small and utilitarian, walls painted white like the door, clearly a front office. It was a bit cluttered, but tidy. A coffee maker and attendant tray of cups, sugar, etc. sat on a low bookcase. A spider plant atop a filing cabinet added a touch of color, and a receptionist's desk bore an old electric typewriter, a mug full of pens and pencils, and a stack of unopened mail.

Mr. Hidalgo led me through a door to a slightly larger office, much more cluttered and homey. Here there were personal touches: pictures on the walls, an ancient cast-iron coat rack with a nice wool jacket hanging on it, a couple of Navajo rugs, and a faint, lingering smell of tobacco.

"This is her," he said, pointing to a small, framed, ancient photograph, one of several grouped on the south wall.

The photo was a portrait of a Latino woman perhaps thirty-five years old, unsmiling (no doubt holding her breath to keep still). She sat facing the camera square on, head erect, shoulders back. Her hair was pulled into a knot on top of her head, and her dress was high-necked and white. Her only adornment was a small locket—or possibly a watch—on a chain, pinned to her dress.

"She's lovely," I said.

"Mm. She had a lot of proposals, some from very prominent men, but she turned them all down. Died an old maid."

"Was she just not interested in marriage?"

"Story goes she was disappointed in love at an early age, but that's all we know. She became a great philanthropist, and of course, a wonderful aunt. A little strange sometimes. She always wore white."

He looked at me with a smile. I smiled back.

"Would you mind if I took a picture of this with my phone?" I asked.

"Go ahead, but don't use the flash, please."

I took out my phone and fiddled with the settings, then took two pictures of the photograph. Turning to Mr. Hidalgo, I said, "Thank you. Do you have any of her papers?"

"Just her diaries. Would you like to see them?"

My heart jumped with excitement. "Yes, please, if it's not too much trouble."

"What makes you so interested in Maria?"

I hesitated, not wanting to show my hand. "I found some references to her in a description of a concert that the original owner of my house also attended."

He nodded. "Oh, yes. She loved music. She even hosted a singing group for a little while." He gestured toward the front office. "Help yourself to coffee. I'll bring the diaries right out."

I smiled and obeyed, going back to the front office to give him privacy. I don't like drinking out of styrofoam but it was the only choice, so I poured a cup and added a spoonful of sugar for comfort. The coffee was tepid, not terribly fresh, but it was strong. I sipped it and strolled to the door, lifting the shade to peek out the only window in the suite. It had a narrow view of the *plazuala*, and if I'd been the resident of that office, I would have kept the shade up so I could see that view.

These small rooms were not what I had imagined for the controller of Hidalgo Plaza, with all its shops and the restaurant and bistro that must bring in a lot of revenue. But then, Mr. Hidalgo wasn't quite what I had imagined either.

"Here you are," said Mr. Hidalgo, returning with his shuffling step and three slender ledgers in his hands. "You can sit at the desk to look at them. Beverly's not here today."

He pushed the mail aside and set the books down. I left my cup on the bookcase and stepped around the desk to the receptionist's chair. "Thank you. This is very kind of you."

He gave a small shrug. "It's nice that you're interested in Maria. I've always been a fan of hers. She kind of got ignored by the family—they weren't happy that she wouldn't marry, you know. She could have made an alliance, and she didn't, and that made them mad. But she did a lot of good, in her own way."

The bell on the door clanked, making us both look up. A tall, gaunt, Hispanic man looked in.

"Eh, 'Duardo!"

Mr. Hidalgo broke into a grin. "Hey, Jose! *Adelante!*"

They went into the back room together, conversing in Spanish. Mr. Hidalgo left the door open, no doubt to keep an eye on me. I turned my attention to the diaries.

They were bound in leather, the pages yellowed but intact. With a little thrill, I recognized Maria's handwriting. Unfortunately, she had written in Spanish. I could understand some of it, but not all.

The oldest of the three volumes was the one that covered the time of Maria's letters to Captain Dusenberry. I flipped through the pages—carefully, so as not to damage them—looking for his name, but I didn't find a single reference. When I reached the last page, I sighed in disappointment. I turned it over and found a picture of La Guadalupana pasted onto inside of the back cover.

I'd always liked Our Lady. I ran a finger lightly over the picture—printed—probably a common piece at the time. I sensed an irregularity and wondered if the print had been raised, or if the fading gold had been painted on by hand. Feeling again, I changed my mind. It wasn't the image, but the paper that felt irregular. The edges were firm, but the center felt softer.

As if there was something behind it.

A tingle ran down my arms. I glanced over my shoulder at the men, who were deep in earnest conversation.

Running my fingertip around the edges of the picture, I found one that was unsecured, the long edge closest to the spine. I swallowed, and gently tried to lift it. I couldn't raise it much, but succeeded enough to see that another piece of paper was behind it.

I looked up at the pencil mug. It held a letter opener. I took it in hand and carefully used it to lift the side of the picture enough that I could slide the paper out.

It was small, old, and folded in half. Holding my breath I opened it.

I instantly recognized the handwriting: it was Captain Dusenberry's.

Mi Corazon –

Catching my breath, I took out my phone, smoothed the brief note open, and took a photo of it with shaking hands. I took two more for insurance, then refolded the note and slid it back into its hiding place after checking that the photos were legible.

My heart was pounding. I glanced at the men again, but they were paying no attention to me.

Looking back at my phone, I saw that it was quarter to noon. I was late.

I put the phone away, returned the letter opener to the mug, and closed the diary. My standing up drew Mr. Hidalgo's attention. I carried the three diaries to the door of his office.

"Pardon me, Mr. Hidalgo. I'm afraid I've got to go. Could I come and look at these again another time?"

He rose and came to accept the books. "Yes, of course."

"Thank you so much." I handed him my card, and another card good for a free cream tea. "You've been very helpful. Thank you for your time."

He saw me out, smiling. I hopped in my car and rushed back to the tearoom, arriving a couple of minutes after noon. Dee was on the way out of the butler's pantry with a tray of tea food as I came in the back door.

"Has Owen arrived?" I asked her.

"Yeah, just now. I sent him to talk to Julio."

I pulled my coat off as I hurried to the kitchen. When I reached it I saw a tableau:

Julio, motionless with a dishtowel in his hands, staring at Owen Hughes with eyes a bit wide.

Owen, camera bag slung over his shoulder, one hand in a pocket, smiling slightly. He had pulled his long, black hair into a ponytail that hung down the back of his black suede coat.

My entering the room broke the spell. Julio turned away to hang up the towel by the sink. Owen turned to me, his smile widening.

"Hi, Ellen."

"Hello! Sorry I wasn't here when you arrived. You've met my chef, Julio Delgado?"

"I have now. Well met," he said, offering a hand to Julio.

"Julio, this is Owen Hughes," I said. "He's a friend of Kris's, and an excellent photographer."

Owen shot me a grin. "Thanks."

Julio shook hands, the clasp lasting a second longer than strictly necessary. "Weren't you at the grand opening?"

"Yes," Owen said. "Did we meet there? I don't remember."

"No, I just remember seeing you. Not many guys with hair like that."

"Oh. Yeah," Owen said, grinning. He glanced toward the windows. "We shooting in here?"

"No," I said, "unless you want to. I thought

one of the alcoves might be a better backdrop. I have two adjacent ones set aside for us."

"Perfect. Lead on."

Julio turned away again, picking up a pair of food storage boxes from the counter. I led him and Owen to the south parlor, where Dahlia and Violet were tucked behind the gift shop. Dee came out of the main parlor as we passed.

"Dee, could you bring a pot of tea to Violet, please?" I said. "Any black – it's for photos."

She nodded and continued down the hall. I had brought a tray of china and accompaniments to Dahlia earlier, ready to set up whatever Owen needed. I had also moved back the screen that usually separated the two alcoves.

"You can use either side," I told him.

"This one, then," he said, stepping into Violet. "This was my favorite at the party. Oh, you've moved the skulls." He looked from the mantel to Vi's portrait.

"Yes," I said, watching Julio set the food boxes on a side table in Dahlia. "New season."

Owen nodded, then turned around. "Can I put my case on a chair?"

"Certainly." I stepped out of his way, and picked up a small plate from the tray. "I thought this, for the food. There are two if you want a second one."

Julio held his hand out for the plate. "Let's start with one."

I moved into Violet to get out of their way. Glancing out the lace sheers over the window, I saw that the wind was picking up. Dry leaves were blowing across the lawn.

"Shall I close the drapes, or leave them open?" I asked.

"Open for now," Owen said, adjusting his camera. "I prefer natural light."

Dee brought in the tea, and a few minutes were spent arranging things on the small table between the two wing chairs in Violet. A fictional setting for two, with filled teacups and the pot in the background of the food plate, where Julio had arranged three scones and half a dozen biscochitos.

Owen shot a couple dozen photos of this, then stood looking at the table, musing. "Let's make it more active," he said, picking up a biscochito and taking a bite. He put the rest back on the plate, and shifted a teacup closer to the bitten cookie as he chewed. These two small changes made the table more intimate, somehow.

"Mm." Owen swallowed. "Oh, man. Best biscochito ever."

"Thanks," Julio said softly.

Owen looked up at him, flashed a smile, then knelt before the table to take more photos. "The food at the party was all great, too."

Julio didn't answer. I glanced at him and saw that he, too, was watching Owen work.

There was a silent undercurrent of intensity in the room. I was fascinated by the small changes Owen made that transformed his subject. I'd had no idea that a table of tea and baked goods could look so different with the addition of a half-folded napkin, or a spoon turned just so, or a scone broken in half on the plate. Julio brought curd and cream and Owen slathered part of the scone, then left the knife beside it as if the user had just been called away.

After a while the afternoon light shifted, making shadows deeper in the room. Owen asked me to build up the fire and close one of the drapes. The remaining daylight still cast shadows, but now the fire's glow added golden touches to the china.

Owen swallowed the tea in a cup and poured fresh, then took photos of the steam rising from the cup. Small details I would never have thought of were like an artist's embellishments in his setting. I had known he was talented, but seeing him work deepened my appreciation of his unfailing eye. I poured tea into a spare cup and stood sipping it as I watched, entranced by the artist at work.

"Excuse me, Ellen?" a voice whispered from the doorway.

I turned to find Iz peeking in. "Yes?"

"Kris wants to know where's the bank bag."

"Oh! It's right here."

I had put my hat and coat on a chair in Dahlia when we came in, and the bag was beneath them. I handed it to Iz, who left with whispered thanks. Her intrusion made me curious about the time, and I checked my phone.

After four. Wow!

"Owen, I hate to bother you, but I think you said you had to be somewhere at five?"

He checked something on his camera and

stood, "Actually, I found out I'm supposed to be here. Kris asked me to come to her, ah, gathering tonight." He glanced toward Julio, who said nothing.

Julio hadn't said much all afternoon, really.

"Oh! I see," I said. "Well, that's fine. Do you think you can get me some photos by tomorrow morning?"

Owen nodded. "I'll make a first cut between now and six-thirty. Can I use this room, or do you need it?"

"No, I blocked it for the whole afternoon. You're welcome to stay."

"Thanks. Guess we're about done, unless there's something else you want to try."

I shook my head. "I think you've found every possible variation. Thank you so much!"

He turned to me, smiling. "It was fun. I love working in your house – such a cool old place."

"Thanks."

He set his camera in its case and picked up the half-scone adorned with cream and curd. With a mischievous glance at me, he ate it. Closing his eyes, he gave a small moan of pleasure.

"I can make you something more substantial if you like," Julio offered quietly. "A sandwich, and we have some soup I could heat up."

Owen opened his eyes, finished chewing, and swallowed. "That would be great. Thanks."

Julio glanced at me. "You don't mind?"

"Of course not. Thanks again, Owen. I'll be upstairs."

He turned his head to smile at me, and nodded. "I'll see if I can pull a couple dozen of the best shots for you."

I smiled back, picked up my coat, and slipped out of the room. Julio followed, walking with me until we reached the staircase. I shot a glance at him as I started up and he continued toward the kitchen. He looked pensive.

I hung my coat on the rack, then peeked into Kris's office. She was putting away the empty bank bag.

"Sorry," I said. "I got distracted. How did the afternoon go?"

She shrugged. "Pretty quiet. You've got a few messages."

She handed me several lavender message slips. I took them to my desk and glanced through them. One from Gina, reminding me about the photo deadline on Friday. One from the Vietnamese job candidate – a polite follow-up. Nothing from Tony.

"I'll be in my suite," I called to Kris as I left and crossed the hall. I put away my hat and coat, and changed into off-duty clothes for the evening. Taking advantage of the privacy, I pulled out my cell phone and checked for text messages. There were none. I kept thinking there was something more to do with my phone, but I couldn't remember what. Attempting to jog my memory, I left it on the kitchenette counter while I put the kettle on for tea.

The impending séance was making me nervous. I'd be glad when it was over, and (somewhat guiltily) I hoped nothing outrageous would happen during the "sitting," as Willow had called it. I had enough ghosts in my life.

Ghosts!

I grabbed my phone and brought up the photos I had taken in Mr. Hidalgo's little office. There was the captain's note to Maria, his neat handwriting slightly hurried (I thought) compared to other samples I'd seen. I went back to my office and downloaded the photos I'd taken of the note and Maria's portrait to my computer, then backed them up on a flash drive to be extra safe.

Bringing up the note on my big screen, I tried to puzzle it out, but my Spanish wasn't equal to the task. *"Corazon"* meant heart: an endearment, and one that a Victorian gentleman would not use with a woman he didn't know well. In fact, I suspected that Captain Dusenberry's using it to address Señorita Hidalgo had not been strictly proper.

Who could I get to translate the note? I wasn't willing to trust just anyone. First of all, I'd taken the photo without Mr. Hidalgo's knowledge or permission. For all I knew, he was unaware of the note's existence. Showing it to any sort of professional, such as Bennett Cole at the Museum of New Mexico, would be opening a can of worms.

Maybe Willow? She'd been able to read the Spanish in Maria's letters. And after all, it was her questioning Captain Dusenberry that had led to my finding the note.

I closed the file and went back to my suite just

as the kettle whistled. With a pot of Keemun steeping, I raided my mini-fridge for something to eat. I didn't have time to cook dinner, so I made a couple of pieces of toast and put some leftover chicken salad between them, then stood munching the sandwich while I gazed out the window and thought about Tia Maria and the captain.

Whatever was in that note, she had kept it as a secret treasure. I was impatient to get it translated, but it would have to wait until after the séance.

TWENTY MINUTES BEFORE 7:00, I emerged and looked into Kris's office. She wasn't there. I slipped into my own office, unlocked the desk, and took out the amethyst pendant Willow had left with me. I felt a little silly putting it on. Woo woo, indeed. Tucking it into my shirt, I locked my desk and headed downstairs, where I peeked into the dining parlor.

Kris was there, putting away the lace tablecloth. The table's floral centerpiece rested on a sideboard; the polished wood was bare, but a couple of candelabra with fresh, white candles stood on the other sideboard, waiting.

I pursed my lips, thinking of dripped wax. Kris would get to clean up any mess, I decided, and went to check the front door.

All was locked, closed, shuttered for the evening. The fires were banked, beds of coals slowly leeching the last of their warmth into the bricks of the chimneys. I looked for Dee, expecting

I might have missed her departure, but I found her in the butler's pantry, looking at her phone. She had not only removed her apron but had changed out of her lavender dress, into jeans and a dark blue sweater that heightened her pale coloring.

"Oh, are you staying?" I asked.

She nodded. "Kris asked me. Does she seem a little tense to you?"

"Yes."

More than.

I continued to the kitchen. Julio and Owen looked up at me from the staff's break table in the far corner, where Owen had been eating supper.

"Julio, did Kris ask for any kind of refreshments?" I asked.

He shook his head.

My inner hostess wouldn't stand for a complete lack of hospitality, so I filled a pitcher with water and put it on a tray with some glasses. This I carried to the main parlor, where I set it on the low table in Rose.

The connecting door between Rose and the dining parlor was open. A glance at the floor told me that the salt Willow had poured across the doorway was largely undisturbed. Stepping over it, I spoke to Kris, who was placing the candelabra so as to illuminate either end of the table.

"Do you want this door open?"

"Yes," she said. "The way it was on Saturday."

I glanced back toward Rose, remembering how the alcove had looked then—draped in black, with the blood-red lanterns casting the only light, while

Gabriel stood there in his golden glory.

The thought came to my mind that Gabriel's wasn't the first death associated with Rose. Maria Garcia, Julio's grandmother, had died there. Right there, in the main parlor, a few steps from the dining parlor.

Stop it, Ellen.

Movement in the hallway outside drew my attention. It was Owen, camera in hand, silently beckoning to me. I joined him, and he started for the stairs.

"Can we download some photos for you?" he asked.

"Yes, please!"

We went up to my office and I turned on my computer. While it was booting, he told me he'd isolated what he thought were the best photos, but that he'd give me the whole set.

"That way if you need more later, you'll have them."

"Thank you so much, Owen. What do I owe you?"

An odd smile curved up one side of his mouth. "Nothing," he said.

"Oh, no you don't." I pulled a notepad toward me and took out a pen. "You're a professional. Tell me your fee, or I'll make one up and send it to you."

He laughed. "OK. I'll send you an invoice."

I looked at him narrowly. "And what about the photos from Saturday? I should pay for those, too."

He shook his head. "Kris already paid me."

"*Kris* did?"

"Gabriel left everything to her."

I sat back, absorbing that. My gaze went to the clock on my computer screen. "It's time to go downstairs," I said.

We disconnected Owen's camera and I shut down the computer, then hurried downstairs after him. Kris was at the back door, having a low-voiced conversation with a pale, brown-haired young man I didn't recognize. Voices drew me to the dining parlor, where Dee stood talking with three other friends of Kris's: Dale (whom I was glad to see), Gwyneth (whom I was surprised to see), and Cherie (whom I was *really* surprised, and not terribly pleased, to see).

Gwyneth, wearing a twilight blue chiffon dress, scurried around the table to envelop me in a jasmine-scented hug. "Ellen! I'm so glad you're going to sit with us."

"You look well," I told her, and meant it. "Is Roberto coming?"

"Oh, no. He doesn't believe in the spirit realm." She smiled. "Yet," she added, with brazen confidence.

I greeted Dale, who looked sharp in a dark gray vest over a black shirt, then turned to face Cherie. She was dressed in a plain black shift, with a long string of tiny black beads around her neck. Her haircut looked even more severe with this ensemble, and she seemed pale and drawn, but (at least) sober.

"How are you?" I asked her.

She ducked her head. "OK," she said quietly.

The lack of drama made me forgive her past behavior. I pressed her hand. "I'm sorry about Gabriel. Are you sure you want to be here?"

She gave me a sidelong glance as she straightened her shoulders, then a single nod. "Yes."

Kris came in, with the pale young man beside her. He was carrying a cardboard box, roughly cubic, about a foot and a half high.

"Everyone, this is Tom," Kris said. "He's going to conduct the session."

Tom nodded in response to a chorus of hellos, and looked rather intently at each of us as Kris ran through our names, as if fixing our faces in memory. He then set his box on a sideboard and opened it, carefully removing what looked like a modern sculpture of polished brass. This he placed in the center of the table, while Kris lit the candelabra.

The others drifted to chairs. I waited near the door, wondering whether I should fetch the extra salt Willow had given me, just in case. Not being able to imagine using it, I didn't bother.

Instead I stared at Tom's apparatus, which he was taking great care to place in the exact center of the table. To my relief, since it incorporated candles, I saw that he had laid out a square of black cloth beneath it.

The gizmo itself was lightweight, and consisted of a ring-shaped base with letters and numbers all around it, four small candle-holders into which Tom placed little white tapers, and a wheel-like top piece that balanced on a point resting in a cup suspended between the candle-holders. The top piece looked a little like a crown, with slanted fan-blades that rode above the candles, and descending from its sides were four points, three of which were short and stout, the fourth being narrow and elongated with a tiny, pointed weight dangling from it on a chain. The point hung about half an inch above the ring with the letters.

I had never seen anything like it. Despite that, it was ringing bells of memory for me. I frowned, staring at it, until I felt someone watching me and looked up into Tom's smiling face.

"It's my own invention," he said softly, his voice deeper than I expected. "It works like those little Christmas decorations with the angels. The heat of the candles makes it turn."

"Right!" I said, remembering. "That's where I've seen it before! We had one when I was a kid."

He nodded, then with a slight smile, beckoned to me. "Join us."

He indicated a chair in the middle of the table, across from his own. I glanced at Kris, but she was already seated at the north end, so I took the empty chair.

Tom handed slips of paper and pencils around. "We're here to attempt to contact Gabriel Rhodes. Please write down any questions you may have for him."

Not expecting this, I sat staring at my blank

slip. I had many questions, but not for Gabriel. I only wished him peace, poor guy.

In the end, I didn't write anything. I gave my paper and pencil back to Tom, who accepted them without comment. Dale hadn't written a question either, but the others had. Dee offered hers to Tom, but he shook his head.

"Please fold it and lay it on the table before you. I'm going to place one of these on each question, to help with clear communication. They're kyanite." He stood and showed us a handful of small greenish crystals, then went around the table setting them on the papers and collecting the pencils, which he put into his box, keeping back one. He took a notepad from the box and turned to Dale. "Would you be willing to record the messages?"

"OK, but I'm not fast," Dale said. "I don't know shorthand."

"You won't need it. The messages will come letter by letter, like this."

Tom touched the crown of his device, and it gently rotated, then drifted to a stop with the pointer hanging above the letter "T."

"Won't it keep rotating while the candles are burning?" I asked.

Tom smiled. "Good question. Yes, until this happens."

He nudged the crown into moving again, then lightly touched the top of a small pin sticking up from the rim as it went by. This made the fan-blades lie flat, and the rotation halted, this time over the letter "U."

"The slightest touch will lower the blades," Tom said. "Then after a second, the candles' heat raises them again." With a gentle finger, he lifted the blades back into place, where they set with a tiny click. "It's designed so that spirits can operate it without expending a lot of energy."

My thoughts snapped back to Willow's explanation of ether. That must be what Tom meant, though he didn't use the word.

"I'll need you to switch places with Cherie, then," Tom said to Dale. "The rest of us will be holding hands."

Dale was sitting on my right. Cherie, who had taken the seat at the south end of the table, traded with him. I gave her a smile meant to reassure as she sat beside me.

Tom set the notepad and pencil before Dale. "Please close your eyes, everyone. Breathe deeply, and release your thoughts of the day. We're looking for a quiet, relaxed state of mind. I'm going to turn out the lights and close the door to the hall, then I'll light the candles in the word wheel."

I closed my eyes, but I couldn't help sneaking peeks at Tom as he moved around the room. Gina's skepticism whispered at me that he could be setting up a way to move the device secretly. Maybe he had magnets that he could manipulate with his knees.

Except brass wasn't magnetic.

Maybe it just *looked* like brass. It could be brass-plated steel.

But that would be heavy. This was paper-thin, and light.

Stop it, Ellen. Just breathe.

I closed my eyes and tried to relax. My thoughts drifted despite my best intentions. I found myself wondering whether Captain Dusenberry was watching this, and what he might think of it. Would he consider it a valid way to communicate, or just a parlor game?

Captain, this is for Kris, to give her closure.

The chandelier went out, sudden darkness sparking a tiny frisson of wonder, until I remembered that Tom was still up. A warmer glow and a whiff of sulfur told me he was lighting the small candle. One last peek through my eyelashes as he sat across from me.

"Everyone but Dale, please place your left hand on the table beside you, palm up," he said.

I complied, then closed my eyes again, hearing the soft sounds of the others' movement.

"Now place your right hand in the hand of your neighbor to the right."

I laid my hand in Cherie's, and felt Gwyneth's hand feather-light in my left. Owen reached across the table to take Cherie's other hand, leaving Dale free to write.

Tom's apparatus was beginning to move. The crown circled slowly, much more slowly than the Christmas angels I remembered. I watch the little pointer glide above the letters.

"Please keep holding hands throughout this session," Tom said, his own hands clasped with

Owen's and Dee's. "It's important that the circle remain closed. Now breathe deeply, and clear your minds. I ask that the guardian angels of everyone at this table watch over us here, and shine their light on us to guard us from darkness."

That was nice. I was beginning to like Tom.

"We are here to reach out to Gabriel Rhodes, who recently crossed into spirit. If he or any of his guardians are here, we ask them to acknowledge our request."

A long silence followed. I watched the wheel turn slowly, hypnotically. My thoughts drifted around as well. I hoped Kris wouldn't be disappointed, hoped Tom was sincere. Wondered what the others had asked Gabriel.

A tiny click, startling because it was unexpected, made me look at the wheel. It had stopped over the letter "O."

I glanced at Tom, who gazed impassively at the device, both hands in his neighbors'. Dale duly recorded the letter. As I looked to the wheel, I saw the blades lifting back into place. Though I knew the heat from the candles was raising them, still I felt a little unnerved.

The wheel moved again, circling a couple of times before stopping on "P." While the blades rose, I wondered why the spirit forces hadn't just moved it over one letter. Perhaps they needed a running start.

More letters clicked into place, while I pondered the physical problems of operating the wheel. Would I have been able to make it stop on a particular letter, just by pressing the pin as Tom had done? Probably not. How, then, could a spirit do so?

Maybe it had been programmed in advance somehow, said the voice of Gina in my head.

"Ophelia," Dale announced.

Kris gave a little gasp, and I thought of the print in her office, depicting the drowned Ophelia from Shakespeare's *Hamlet*. I didn't think Tom had been up there. My impression was that this was his first visit to the tearoom.

The wheel moved again, stopping on "N," then "O."

"No," Dale said.

I glanced at Kris. She swallowed, biting her lip.

The wheel moved to "D," followed by a period. I looked at Dee.

The wheel continued spelling. "Yes," Dale said as the final letter clicked into place.

Dee nodded, eyes on the wheel.

Next was "Cher," which I guessed was short for "Cherie." The little sob she gave seemed to confirm this. The message she received was "Yes," which evoked a larger sob.

This seemed much more clinical and less mysterious than I had expected. None of the yes-or-no messages made sense to me, but they seemed to make sense to the recipients. I watched Tom, but he never moved, his gaze remaining on the wheel. I wondered if he had gone into some kind of trance.

"Owen" was followed by a much longer

message: "Awesome," which made Owen laugh. Next the wheel spelled out "N-E-T-H," then paused.

I felt Gwyneth shift beside me. Dale frowned at his notes, and said, "Neth?"

"Oh!" Gwyneth said, "It's me." She began to cry, and the wheel turned.

I followed as the letters were spelled out: "L-E-T-G-O." Dale announced softly, "Let go."

I glanced at Gwyneth, who gave a ragged sigh and nodded.

The wheel turned for a long while without stopping. Just as I began to wonder whether the session was over, it clicked to a stop on "E."

I watched, my nape prickling, as the letters of my name followed.

"Ellen," Dale announced.

I hadn't written a question. I glanced up at Tom. He showed no reaction.

"Valid," Dale said, when that word was spelled.

The prickling traveled down my spine as the wheel began to move again. It spelled out "attic," then "N-E-"

To my right, Cherie gave a little gasp. "Look!"

She was staring up at the chandelier. More gasps followed as the others looked up.

One crystal drop was swaying gently back and forth.

Hello, Captain.

6

WE WAITED EXPECTANTLY, but no more letters came. I realized I was holding my breath, and let it out in a long sigh. Had Cherie's outburst interrupted the message intended for me? Or maybe the spirits had run out of steam?

After a minute, Tom announced that the session had ended. He said something about thanking the spirits and wishing Gabriel well, but my attention was on the women to either side of me, both softly crying. When Tom gave us permission to release hands, I quietly stood and fetched the tray of water, handing glasses around the table.

No one spoke. My own feelings were rather tumultuous. Unless Dale had somehow reached into my thoughts for the rather unusual word, "valid," the séance had been genuine, and Captain Dusenberry had been present as well as Gabriel.

I returned to my chair with a glass of water and sipped it, letting that thought sink in. Across the table from me, Tom sat with eyes closed.

Communing? Resting?

What Willow had told me about ether implied that Tom had allowed the spirits to draw on his personal store of that stuff in order to move the wheel. Despite his ingenious device, it would still have cost him something, and the process of spelling out messages letter by letter had taken some time.

As if aware of my regard, Tom opened his eyes. He gave me a slight smile, then looked around the table.

"Does anyone wish to share their question? It's optional, of course."

A moment's silence, then Dee raised her hand. "I will."

Tom nodded to her, and Dee picked up her folded paper, setting the kyanite crystal to one side. "I asked, 'Have you forgiven Monica?'"

Someone gasped.

"And the answer was 'Yes,'" Dale said, consulting his notes.

Dee smiled slightly, and offered her page to Tom. He shook his head.

"Hand it to someone else, please, so they can verify. I don't touch the questions."

"I'll take it," Kris said. Dee placed the paper in her hand. Kris read it, then nodded. "My question was, 'Did you jump?'"

"Oh!" Gwyneth squeaked, dabbing at her eyes with a handkerchief I hadn't seen her produce.

"He meant me when he said 'Ophelia,'" Kris added.

Dale consulted his notes. "The answer was 'No,'" he said. Kris glanced at Gwyneth, then gave her slip to Dee to confirm.

"Well," Owen said after a moment. "I wasn't so serious. I asked what it was like being dead." He looked at me with an impish grin.

Dale kept a straight face. "The answer was 'Awesome.'"

I couldn't help laughing softly, and heard someone else do the same. I could just imagine Gabriel saying that. The tension at the table seemed to relax a little as Owen handed his question to Dale, who read it and nodded.

"Oh, well," Gwyneth said, dabbing her cheeks. "I asked how he wanted to be remembered."

Dale shifted and looked down at the notepad. "He answered, 'Let go.'"

"He *would*." Gwyneth said, and blew her nose.

"He called you 'Neth?'" Dale asked.

Gwyneth nodded, sniffling. "He used to call me that to make me mad. Only in private." She shot an apologetic glance at Kris, who gave a wry smile.

Gwyneth handed her page to me. I read it, confirming the question with a nod.

Cherie was the only one with a question still before her. I turned my head slightly, watching her. Everyone waited.

"You can keep your question private," Tom said.

Cherie took a deep breath. "No, I'll share. I asked if he forgave me."

"For what?" Gwyneth asked, with impulsive

sympathy.

Cherie shrugged, sighing. "Everything."

"He answered, 'Yes,'" Dale said. Cherie handed him her question, and he read it, nodding.

I felt Tom's gaze on me.

"I didn't ask a question," I said.

Tom nodded. "You got a message, though. But not from Gabriel, I think."

"No, I think not." I cleared my throat. "Earlier, I was thinking about Captain Dusenberry—you know about him?"

Tom nodded.

"Yes. Well, I was wondering what he would think of all this." I gestured to the wheel. "I wondered whether he would consider this a valid method of communication."

"Valid?" Dale said quickly. "That's the word you had in mind?"

"Yes. So apparently he chose to answer that question."

"And he moved the chandelier crystal so you would know it was him," Cherie said.

"Probably," I said.

"So cool," Dee whispered.

I shot her a look. It would have been cooler if the message had been complete. "Valid, attic, ne-" wasn't much to go on. If "ne" was the start of "near," then it could have been the beginning of a reference to some point upstairs. Maybe the captain wanted me to look for something up there. More letters, perhaps? But without the rest of the message, I'd have to search the whole upper floor.

That could take a while.

I picked up my water glass. It was empty.

"Would anyone like some tea?"

⁓

Dee joined me in the butler's pantry, taking down one of the larger teapots while I boiled water and chose a tea to brew. Not wanting something too heavy that late in the evening, I decided on oolong.

"That's so cool that you got a message from the captain!" Dee said, stacking cups and saucers on a tray.

"Please, *do not* mention any of this to Mrs. Olavssen."

"No way," Dee said, eyes wide. "She'd want to get Tom to do it again!"

"Exactly."

"You're going to tell Willow, though—right?"

The kettle boiled, and I picked it up. "Yes. She knew we were doing this."

"What about Detective Aragón?"

I paused with the kettle in hand. The question had produced a little stab of pain. "I don't know," I said, and poured the water into the teapot. The flowery aroma of oolong rose into the air.

"Go ahead and take those out," I said. "I'll bring this when it's ready."

I leaned against the counter, drinking in the fragrance of the steeping tea while I thought about Dee's question. It had been several days since Tony had responded to any of my messages. Sure, he might be busy, but I was beginning to get the feeling that he wasn't going to respond. Ever.

Was it time to face the possibility that my interference (as he called it) in his investigation of Gabriel's death had destroyed our personal relationship?

I shied away from the thought, telling myself it was too soon. Tony was busy, or he was angry but would eventually forgive me. I rebuilt all my little defensive beliefs, because I wasn't ready to give them up.

And that told me something right there. I couldn't bear to think of losing Tony.

Detective Arrogant, as I had once called him, had worked his way into my heart despite his many deficiencies of common courtesy. I had learned that it wasn't arrogance (usually), but uncertainty, behind his occasional rudeness. And beneath the arrogant appearance and the some-time lack of confidence, he had a gentle heart.

His job was unpleasant, to say the least. He had once described it to me as cleaning up other people's messes. He could have chosen something else, but he was proud of his work, and he knew he was doing good.

I wanted to support that. I had never meant to cross him. I knew that he cared about justice, and I had pursued justice in my own way, hoping that I was helping him.

But he hadn't seen it that way.

The timer went off, and I lifted the infuser from the teapot, then set the lid on the pot and carried it to the dining parlor. The word wheel was still, its candles extinguished, and the chandelier was on. The mood in the room was more relaxed, as people quietly chatted.

Dee had given everyone a teacup. I went around the table, pouring. When I reached Tom, he shook his head.

"No thanks," he said with a smile.

"Would you like a tisane? Something without caffeine?"

"Just some more water would be great."

"I'll get it," Dee said, and darted out.

I poured tea for everyone else, then sat with my cup, sipping and savoring the oolong, enjoying the warmth of the cup in my hands. Kris and Gwyneth were talking about Gabriel in low, earnest tones, and Dale and Owen were discussing the upcoming ski season.

To my right, Cherie sat staring into her cup. I turned to her.

"Was this helpful?"

She swallowed. "Yes. I just wanted to ... I was so out of it, that night, and then I never saw him again." She wiped away a tear and picked up her cup, then met my gaze. "Dale's bugging me to go to AA."

"Dale?" I glanced at him across the table, but he hadn't heard.

"Yeah, his dad's a recovered alcoholic. He's all hypersensitive about it."

"Are you considering going?" I asked gently.

Cherie hunched a shoulder. "I might. Just to shut him up." She sipped her tea and put the cup down. It rattled a little in the saucer.

I hoped she would decide to go, but I didn't dare say so. She seemed both fragile and brittle, and I didn't want to create resistance. I didn't know her well enough to offer advice.

My gaze shifted to Dale, and I realized the scales had tipped. Not only was he intelligent, well-mannered, and dressed with quiet elegance, he had a kind heart and was willing to go out of his way for a friend. What I'd seen of him, tonight and previously, combined with what Cherie had just told me, made me want to have him on my staff.

Dee came back with a pitcher of water and filled everyone's glasses. I drank half of mine at once, surprised at how thirsty I felt. Tom also drank deeply, then stood and fetched his box, and started dismantling the word wheel.

The others took this as the signal to depart. They got up, exchanging hugs, saying goodbye. There was a softness in the room now, where there had been tension before. That, alone, was worth the effort.

Dale brought Cherie her coat, and I gathered that he had given her a ride. As they went out together I wondered, not for the first time, if there was anything between them. I didn't think so. I didn't sense any sexual tension there. They seemed to be just friends.

Owen sought me out to say good night. "Thanks for hosting this. It was great!"

"Thanks again for the photos. Remember to bill me," I said, walking with him to the back door.

Gwyneth came up behind us, swathed in a floor-length, white fur coat. It was fake fur, I realized, but still amazing.

"Thank you, Ellen!" she said, wrapping me in a silky-warm hug.

"Good to see you," I told her, meaning it. I liked her.

I was getting to like all of Kris's friends, really. Even Cherie.

"May I escort you to your chariot, milady?" Owen said, offering her an arm. Gwyneth giggled and took it.

As I closed the door after them, Kris came out of the parlor, looking tired. All her nervous tension was gone.

"My coat's upstairs," she said, turning away.

I went with her to the foot of the stairs. "Did you get what you wanted?"

She paused with a foot on the bottom step, tilting her head. "I think so," she said. "Yes."

She gave me a wan smile, then headed up. With her footsteps fading overhead, I went back to the dining parlor, where I found Tom carefully packing away the pieces of his word wheel, the kyanite crystals piled beside him. Dee was collecting teacups and water glasses onto a tray.

"Shall I stay and wash these?" she asked.

"No, leave them in the kitchen. Mick can do them in the morning."

When she'd gone out with the tray, I turned to Tom. "Congratulations. You've convinced me."

He smiled slightly, shaking his head. "No.

You've made a decision, based on the evidence you've observed. It's what we do."

"Pretty compelling evidence."

He scooped up the crystals, put them into the box, then folded the top shut. "Thanks for providing the space. I was glad to be here, after all I've heard about this house. You've got some wonderful friends."

"Well, they're Kris's friends."

He shook his head, smiling. "I mean the captain and your other friends."

"There's more than one?" I said, alarmed.

His smile widened. "We all have many friends and family watching over us on the other side. You're no exception. Your friends are quite interesting, though. I was glad to have the chance to work with them."

Interesting? I wasn't sure I wanted to know what he meant.

"May I ask you a question?" I said.

"Sure."

"If you can communicate with spirits, why do you need that?" I pointed to the box.

"The wheel? Oh, it's not for me. It's for you."

"Me?"

"All of you. We all base our decisions and beliefs on evidence. The wheel provides that. Seeing it spell out messages that only you understand gives you confirmation. Right?"

I nodded slowly. "Right."

Ophelia. The word "valid." Gwyneth's nickname of "Neth," which she'd said was private between her and Gabriel. Evidence upon evidence. Too much to be coincidence.

"Do you ever have doubts?" I asked.

"Me? Every day." He picked up his box. "It's part of being human. We have to have things proved to us over and over again, and even then we doubt."

I went with him to the hall and watched him put on his coat. Kris came downstairs, and Dee came out of the side hall. We all said goodbye at the back door, and I locked it after them, then stood in the hall listening to them get into cars and drive away.

Doubt. Yes, there it was, still niggling. Still wondering if Tom could somehow have found out about all these secret things, or made lucky guesses, and through some trickery I couldn't imagine sent it all through his word wheel.

Or was it, as I hoped in my secret heart, truly real?

Tom had called the captain my friend. I wanted that to be true, almost as much as I wanted to hear from Tony again.

As if in answer to my thoughts, the piano began to play.

I stood motionless, listening, hardly daring to breathe. As before, it was just a melody, single notes picked out one by one. Was the captain borrowing my ether to do this? If so, I couldn't feel it.

The notes were familiar, a little halting, but I was able to catch and recognize the melody. It was

"Contessa, Perdono" from *The Marriage of Figaro* again. This time he played the phrase that followed the one he had played months ago. I softly sang along.

—*io sono, e dico di sì.*

I am gentler, and say yes.

About the Author

photo by Chris Krohn

PATRICE GREENWOOD was born and raised in New Mexico, and remembers when the Santa Fe Plaza was home to more dusty dogs than trendy art galleries. She has been writing fiction longer than she cares to admit, perpetrating over twenty published novels in various genres. She uses a different name for each genre, thus enabling her to pretend she is a Secret Agent.

She loves afternoon tea, old buildings, gourmet tailgating at the opera, ghost stories, costumes, and solving puzzles. Her popular Wisteria Tearoom Mysteries are colored by many of these interests. She is presently collapsed on her chaise longue, sipping Wisteria White tea and planning the next book in the series.

Made in the USA
Middletown, DE
18 August 2017